THE FOREIGNER

MAURICE R. BELFONTE

Edited by Kristen Corrects, Inc.
Cover art design by Joshua Jadon

First edition published 2017

ISBN-13: 978-0692959411
ISBN-10: 0692959416

Library of Congress Control Number: Available Upon Request

Visit www.itstimenow.org

TABLE OF CONTENTS

DEDICATION

To Mom - I miss you more than words can express.

To my wife and my son, and to my family and friends who encouraged me along the way.

Thank you.

"There is greatness on the inside of you. My hope is that you realize that greatness and live the life you've always dreamed of."

- Maurice R. Belfonte

CHAPTER ONE
CAMP

"I'm going to miss the bus to camp if we don't leave in the next five minutes, Mom," I said. "Are you almost ready?"

"Almost, Michael. I just need two more minutes."

I rolled my eyes, knowing that meant ten more minutes.

"Hey!" she said. She was glaring at me from the bathroom. "I saw that. I said I'll be ready in two minutes. Go put everything in the car and wait for me."

"Can I start it up?" I asked with a wide grin.

She sighed. "Yes, Michael. Start up the car."

"Yeah baby!" I shouted.

"And say bye to your sister!" Mom yelled as I ran out the door.

I grabbed the keys and sprinted down the hall to Nicky's room.

"Nicky! Nicky!" I yelled.

"What do you want, Michael? Can't you see I'm listening to my music?"

"I'm not blind. I'm just saying goodbye! I'm off to camp."

She scoffed, then turned and looked at me with her dark eyes. "*Finally.* Now I can get some time to myself without having to worry about taking care of you."

My big sister's attitude wouldn't bring me down. "Whatever! I'm outta here. See ya!"

Even though I couldn't drive, starting up the car was thrilling enough. It had a roar to it, like a sports car. Even though it was certainly not one. It was an old white hatchback with a tan interior. There were a couple of holes in the muffler, which most likely made it roar the way it did. It had a good stereo system and thankfully the air conditioning worked. That's all that mattered to my mother.

"I'm all set! Let's get you to that bus, champ."

Mom always called me champ because of all the medals and trophies I'd won in swimming. Even though my father wasn't there, the one thing he made sure he took care of was paying for those lessons. I'd been doing it since I was about four years old. And now, ten years later, I had accumulated over fifty medals and twenty trophies.

"All right, off we go." Mom looked at me in the passenger seat. "Are you excited?"

"Of course I am. I'm just glad we all made it in again. You know Kevin almost missed the deadline? He's lucky Danny decided to be a counselor this year, or he might not have made it."

Danny had been one of the camp counselors ever since we started going three years ago. He was like the cool older brother none of us had. We had all grown up in the same neighborhood in Trinidad and our families knew each other well. Danny was our inside connection at the camp. He did everything he could to make sure that we all got in, as there was always a waiting list.

"What about your other friends? Did they make the deadline?"

"Yup! Ashley, Johnny, and Tony registered weeks ago."

Mom grinned. "Perfect! I'm sure you guys will have lots of fun," She looked in the rear view mirror as she started backing out of the garage. "What are you looking forward to the most?"

"Those cooking lessons we get twice a week," I answered without hesitation.

Mom hit the brakes and looked at me. "Really? You're not looking forward to soccer, or arts and crafts, or even the tennis lessons? Those are all things you love and are good at. Not to mention swimming."

"Yeah I know. But I really like the cooking. I have to make sure I learn as much as I can if I'm going to keep up with the best cook in the world."

"Oh yeah?" She arched an eyebrow. "And who is that?"

"You, of course!"

She grinned and continued backing the car out. "Well thank you, son. That means a lot to me."

"Maybe one day we can open a restaurant together. We'll cook all the food and Nicky can take the orders and handle the money. We'll call it Taste of The Island. It'll be the best restaurant in Trinidad." I said.

Mom and I laughed, mostly at the idea that we would be having fun cooking, while Nicky got to do all the hard work up front.

"That sounds like a plan." Mom said.

"She definitely has no business in the kitchen. She can't even boil rice," I added.

Mom joined me in a soft chuckle as we turned down the block where the bus was waiting.

"That's not nice!" She said, shaking her head.

"But you're laughing."

"Okay," she agreed. "It was a little funny. But let's not tell Nicky." She looked at me seriously. I knew she would keep our secret.

I made a zipping motion across my mouth, to show our secret was safe and sound.

"There's the bus!" She said, looking forward.

"Just in time."

She parked on the side of the road. "Now you remember the rules, right?"

"Yes, Mom. No fighting, no cursing, no fooling around, be respectful, be kind, and have fun," I recited.

"One more!"

"Call you every day."

"Perfect!"

"Hey Michael, come on," Kevin said, his voice muffled through the car's passenger side window. "It's almost time to go. I saved you a seat next to me."

"Hello Kevin!" Mom waved.

"Oh hi, Mrs. B."

Mom turned to me and said quietly, "I know we haven't been spending as much time together as we usually do since I got that promotion at the airport." Her eyes searched mine. "But I promise, when you get home from camp I will make more time for you and your sister."

A smile grew on my face. "That'll be awesome!"

She nodded. "Okay. Let me help you with your stuff."

Danny approached as Mom hauled my bag out of the trunk. "Hi, Mrs. B," he said to her. "How are you?"

She looked up, happy to see him. "Oh hi, Danny. I just got a promotion at the airport so things are very busy. In fact, I have to get going. Looks like you are about to take off too," she said, looking at the bus, which was already full of loud and excited teens.

She hugged me. "I love you, Michael. Be good."

"*Mom*," I said, struggling to get out of her arms.

"Nope," she said, holding on tight to me, "I'm not leaving until I get a real hug from you."

"Mom, my friends are gonna see—"

Then I heard it.

"Michael's a momma's boy!"

I arched my neck to look up at the school bus. There were all my friends, laughing and pointing as my mom hugged me.

"*Mom*!"

"Oh, all right," she said, finally releasing me. "You know, one day I'm not going to be around anymore, then you're sure gonna wish you hugged me more often." She wagged a finger at me.

This only riled up my friends more.

"OHH! MICHAEL!" they shouted, even louder now. "Michael's in trouble with his mom!"

Mom turned to Danny, a grin on her face. "Take care of my boy."

Danny smiled. "You got it, Mrs. B," he said with a nod.

"Bye, Michael," she said to me as she walked to the car. "I love you!"

I turned away from the bus so my friends couldn't hear me. "Love you too," I mumbled. As I boarded the bus Danny handed me a folder with some forms in it. We always got them. The most important things were the list of rules and who was going to be my roommate for the next few weeks. I couldn't focus on reading them now though. All I wanted was to get seated so that everyone would stop making fun of me.

***

After a two-hour bus ride, we finally arrived at the camp. We always looked forward to coming here during summer break. Pulling up to the front was always a pleasant sight. Some big-shot in the oil industry had bought the property and turned it into one of the biggest and best sleepover campsites in the country. He'd spent a lot of time and money making it into something spectacular. The front gates stood at least twenty feet tall, while a long tree-lined road led up to the dorms. The grounds were immaculately kept and manicured to a T. It was certainly a warm and welcoming place for us to spend the next few weeks.

The bus rolled to a stop in front of the brightly painted dorms. Danny stood at the front of the bus. "Okay, everyone. For those of you who may not know me, my name is Danny. I am the lead counselor this year. Are you all ready to have a good time?"

"Yeah!" The resounding response made the bus vibrate.

Danny appeared impressed at our noise. "Not bad, guys. Let's unload the bus and get everything up to our assigned rooms. In thirty minutes everyone meet in the courtyard, so we can discuss what you'll be doing this summer."

Danny was strict about time, so we knew we had to hustle. As it turned out, Kevin and I were rooming together; Johnny was with Tony, and Ashley was on the other side of the camp with the girls.

We arrived in the courtyard on time, just as Danny was starting his speech. He stood in the center of the courtyard and addressed all 125 of us.

"Because this is your first day here, we don't really have anything scheduled—just settle in and get to know everyone. The mess hall is over there"—he pointed to the building behind him—"and dinner is at six o'clock sharp." He told us the ground rules, but it was nothing we hadn't heard before. Curfew is at ten o'clock. Breakfast is at eight. Daily activities start at nine every day.

"That's it, guys," he said. "Break!"

For the first three days, everything was great.

And then it happened.

CHAPTER TWO
THE TAKEOVER

"Drop everything you're doing, pack your bags, and get to the mess hall as quickly as possible," Danny said as he burst into the room. "Something terrible has happened."

I was shocked to see him so rattled. He was usually so cool, calm, and collected, but not now.

I glanced at the others. Tony, and Johnny were playing cards on the floor. They looked stunned. Kevin was sitting on the bunk next to me, looking nervous.

I sat up quickly, but kept my composure. After all, I was the leader of the group, I had to at least look and sound confident.

"What's happened, Danny? What's going on?"

"Everything will be explained in the mess hall," Danny said, motioning toward the door. "Now come on, get downstairs. I have to make sure everyone is out of their rooms."

We'd been up since dawn for our workout and daily run. We were exhausted and the last thing we wanted to do was move fast. Besides, what could be so serious that we would all have to rush down to the mess hall?

I climbed down the bunk's ladder, careful not to move too quickly. I could feel my friends' eyes on me. Watching. Waiting to see how I would react. They all looked up to me. I had to play it cool, even in this strange situation. I couldn't let my guard down and show them just how nervous I was inside.

The others followed me as I walked toward the door. Danny kept his eye on us.

"Whatever this is, it sounds serious," Tony muttered, once we were outside in the fading light. The sun was setting over the ocean, throwing an orange haze over the camp. Everywhere, people were running and shouting.

"I'm starting to feel a little nervous," Tony said. He looked at me worriedly. "What about you, Mike?"

What were all those people running for? What was going on? My heart thumped in my ears and I could feel my chest tightening. Should we be running too?

"Mike?" Tony asked again.

I blinked—back to reality. Tony, Johnny, and Kevin were staring at me, wondering what to do next. I smiled at them and scoffed. "I'm not too worried," I lied. "Nothing could be that serious." I turned back to the center of camp, so the others couldn't see my face or my nervousness. I couldn't let the other guys know how I was really feeling.

"A little bit faster, Michael," Danny prompted from behind us. I was still standing on the steps of the cabin, blocking the way.

I stepped down into the sandy dirt. Counselors ran from cabin to cabin, ushering students out. Shouts rose, creating an uproar that was very different from the normal raucousness of the camp. Nearby, a large group was frantically exiting their cabin.

"Hey," I called to them. "What's going on?"

One of them looked over at me and shrugged. "I heard the military is involved."

I frowned. "The military? They only show up when something really big happens."

"This must be pretty serious," Kevin murmured behind me.

"Guys," Danny said, "to the mess hall. *Now.*" He turned away to instruct another group.

We followed everyone else towards the mess hall, which was bound to be packed full of all the students in the camp. All we could hear were the counselors yelling at their groups, trying to keep everyone as organized as possible.

I searched the crowd for faces. I'd always kept a close circle of friends—it was easier to be in charge when there were only a few people who looked up to you. But there was one person in particular I was searching for.

I finally saw Ashley standing in the middle of the courtyard looking lost and confused. Somehow she must have gotten separated from her group. I had to help her.

"Ashley. Ashley!" I yelled.

She turned, a lost look on her face. Her cheeks were red and her eyes were filled with tears. It looked like she was trying to say something. But she was so afraid she couldn't utter a word.

"Ashley. Come on." I pushed my way through the crowd towards her. "Why are you just standing there like that?"

She opened her mouth to speak, but nothing came out.

"Come on, Michael, forget about her," Johnny said, grabbing my arm. "She's got her own group that can take care of her."

I wrenched my arm out of his grip. "She's not with her group right now." I glared at him. "We have to help her."

The others looked hesitant. "I don't know, Michael," Johnny replied. "Danny said we should get to the mess hall as quickly as possible. We should go with everyone else, now. Let one of the counselors take care of her."

I rounded on him. "Are you crazy? That's our friend. We have to help her."

"Yeah Johnny," Tony said. "We can't just leave her. That would be messed up."

Johnny scoffed. "Well I don't want to get in any trouble for doing anything other than what we were told. So I'm going."

I punched him in the shoulder. "Punk! Go ahead then."

"Michael—" Ashley started.

"Leave, Johnny," Kevin said. "Just go."

I balled my hands into fists, glaring at Johnny. It was a good thing Kevin was here. He always had my back. Johnny turned and walked off.

"Ashley, come on. Everything is going to be fine. But we have to get to the mess hall. Take my hand and follow us, okay?" I said.

I couldn't believe how much she was shaking. I could hear her teeth chattering. And her hands were freezing. Ashley was definitely more scared than I thought.

"Excuse me, excuse me, coming through. Move it people, move it!" I yelled. I wanted to get to the mess hall as fast as possible. I hadn't had this much adrenaline pumping through me for a very long time, not even during our morning exercises. My arms and legs thrummed with energy. I felt like I could probably scale a fence in one leap.

As we shoved our way past the other students to the mess hall, I could see some of the counselors standing at the entrance. I picked out Danny off to the left. Johnny was standing next to him. I started to go to the other side, but Ashley took the lead and marched up to Johnny.

"You jerk!" she said, and shoved him.

"Whoa!" Danny shouted. "Ashley, no violence!"

Ashley ignored him, going at Johnny more aggressively. "How could you leave me like that? I thought we were friends!"

Johnny scoffed. "Chill out, Ashley! Danny told us to get here as quickly as possible. I was just trying to follow instructions."

"You're full of it," she spat. "We never leave anyone behind, remember? That's our pact." She pointed a finger at him. "If you ever do that to me again, our friendship is over."

"Okay, okay, I'm sorry! Sheesh!" Johnny said, putting his hands up.

The volume in the mess hall was immense. People were crying, others were just yelling across the room trying to find out what was happening, and some were just sitting around in circles consoling one another until they got some information. Several minutes passed as the last of the students made their way into the hall.

"Attention everyone! May I have your attention please?" Danny said over a loudspeaker at the front of the room. "What we are about to show you is very scary and very serious. I need you all to try to remain as calm as possible until we can be sure that the situation is under control."

The room went quiet. Whatever this was, it was a big deal.

The sound of wheels squeaking made everyone turn their heads. One of the counselors was rolling in a big TV from the classroom next door. People began mumbling softly to one another, creating a hum in the room. I looked around and saw the kid who had told me the military was involved. Was that true?

A hush fell over the room when Miss Jan, the other counselor, put the TV on. All eyes were fixed on the screen, and then, there it was. The reason we had all been rushed down here.

"Ladies and gentlemen, as of 6'oclock this evening, the government of Trinidad and Tobago has been overthrown. We are asking everyone to remain calm. Revolutionary forces have taken control of the streets."

These were the words of the rebel leader who had taken control of the country. He and his followers had placed the Prime Minister and his staff under arrest. So far, no one had been able to make it out of the building.

This was why everyone was in such a panic. It seemed unreal. Our government had been overthrown.

I never would have thought that someone could take over an entire country. But this guy and his army did just that.

As the initial shock wore off, students started asking questions. The room erupted into a loud roar as everyone began talking at once.

Miss Jan rushed to turn the TV off while the rebel leader continued to speak.

"Did you guys see his face?" I asked Kevin and Tony. "He looks menacing, like he would hurt you at the drop of a dime."

"Yeah, and did you see those guys standing behind him with the big guns?" Kevin said. "They definitely looked really mean and dangerous." He shifted on his feet. "I don't like this, you guys. I don't like this at all."

"I don't think any of us do, Kev," said Tony.

At the front of the room, Danny had started using the loudspeaker again. "Many of your parents are on the way. Just sit tight until we get this figured out."

"We're all sitting ducks until our parents get here," Ashley said.

We had no idea how we were getting out of here. I didn't know if my mother was on her way, and the others didn't know about their parents either.

Suddenly, I felt a deep vibration through the soles of my feet and could hear a deep rumbling sound. I stopped to see if I could figure out what was causing it.

"Maybe we should—" Kevin started.

"Shh!" I interrupted. "Do you guys hear that?"

Ashley looked at me. "Hear what, Michael? What are you talking about?"

"Shh! Listen, that noise. It sounds like a lot of trucks. They're getting louder. Looks like that kid was right after all."

Ashley shook her head. "Can we stop talking about this please?" she said nervously. "I just want to know when my parents are getting here."

"Yeah, I want to know the same thing. We should go ask Danny. Come on!" I said.

As we scrambled through the frantic crowd to find Danny, government soldiers began flooding the hallways, checking all the rooms to make sure all the kids were out. They had come from an army base far out East to try to regain control of the situation. They were definitely moving as if we were in a state of emergency. No words, just hand signals. Their guns were drawn and they wore bulletproof vests.

Things were escalating fast. We needed to get some answers.

We came up behind Danny, who was talking to who seemed like the officer in charge.

"But I don't understand! How are we supposed to get all of these kids out of here and to their homes in only a few hours? We haven't even heard from all of their parents yet," Danny said.

"That's not my problem, sir. All I know is the curfew will go into effect at twenty two hundred hours, not a second later. Anyone found outside of their homes after that time will be arrested. That is a promise from the rebel leader."

I felt the color drain from my face.

Ashley turned to me, panic etched in her expression. "Did that army guy just say there is going to be a curfew set for 10:00 and if we are caught outside after that we will be arrested?"

I glanced at my watch. It was 6:45.

It seemed as though the world had slowed down. I could feel my heart beating in my chest, and my shoulders rise and fall with every breath I took. How precious it all seemed now. In a matter of hours, I might be behind bars.

Ashley couldn't hold it together for another second. She burst into tears.

I was still trying to be strong and act like nothing was affecting me, but that was getting harder and harder to do. This situation just seemed too extreme. These goons were shutting down our entire country.

"I just want to go home. I just want my dad to come and pick me up," Ashley sobbed.

Danny turned around, hearing Ashley's sobs. "What are you guys doing here?" He must have seen the expression on our faces, because he asked, "Were you listening to our conversation? How much of it did you hear?"

"We heard enough to know that we could be prisoners in three hours if we don't make it home," I said.

"Have you heard from any of our parents?" Kevin asked.

Danny shook his head. "I haven't yet. Let's go to the main office now and see if we can get a hold of them."

I grabbed Ashley's hand, yanking her behind me as we followed Danny to the main office. It was only two doors down but seemed like a mile away. Getting through all the soldiers, counselors, and kids was just crazy.

When we finally made it to the office, the line was already out of the door. Everyone was scrambling to get in contact with someone, anyone. At this point it didn't matter if it was a parent or not. As long as they could come and pick us up.

Thirty minutes later, we stepped up to the phone.

"I think Ashley should go first," I said.

"Thanks Michael." Ashley's eyes were red and puffy. She hesitated. "I'm not sure if I should call my house or my dad's job first."

"Try calling the house, Ashley," Danny said. "You might have better luck reaching someone there since this has been going on for a while now. I'm sure most people made their way home as soon as the news broke."

Ashley dialed. We all waited.

"Hello! Mom?" Ashley said. A smile immediately spreading across her face. "Okay, Mom. The military has the entire site on lockdown! Everywhere you look, there's a green uniform. And they all have their guns out like they're ready for battle or something. They're trying to get everyone out of here even though some of the other kids haven't spoken to their parents yet. Are things really that bad out there? Are these people really that dangerous? I'm scared."

She was silent as her mom spoke on the other end.

"Okay, Mom. I will! I love you too."

"So? What did she say?" I asked.

She hung up the phone and then looked at me. "Mom said that since the takeover, the situation has gotten worse, but that I shouldn't worry. My dad's already on the way here." She passed the phone to me.

I knew my mother was at work at the airport, but I almost never got through to her when I called the office. Her cell phone would go in and out of service while she was there for some reason. So that would be no good. My dad was out of the country on business, as usual. I sighed, frustrated. I dialed the number of my mom's office.

Someone picked up the phone, but there was so much noise on the other end of the line, I couldn't tell who it was.

"Hello. Can I please speak with Sue? This is her son, Michael," I shouted.

"Hey, Michael. Your mother has been worried sick. Let me get her for you."

I sighed, feeling the stress lessen slightly. "Thank you."

"Michael! Are you there? Michael?"

"Mom. I'm here, Mom."

"Jesus! Are you okay? What's going on there? I haven't been able to get a call through at all."

"It's pure chaos. The army is here and they look like they're ready to go to war. Every single one of them has their guns out. Are the rebels coming here or something? Why did they send the military here?"

She hesitated. "I'm not sure how to answer that, son. I just know I need to get you out of there. I can't leave the office right now though, so I asked your uncle to pick you up. He should be there shortly with your sister."

"Thank God! I can't wait to get out of here and go home where it's safe."

"No, Michael. You're not going home. You're coming here."

"Why would I come to the airport?"

"I'm doing everything I can to get you and your sister out of the country. I'm sending you both to New York to stay with your Aunt Sandy and Uncle Carl."

"What? Wait. Mom. New York? You can't send us to New York. Why can't we just go home? Or to Uncle Dave's house?" My world was unraveling. Ashley, Kevin, and Tony looked at me with wide eyes, listening intently.

"It may not be safe enough, Michael. If this guy on TV is serious about what he is saying then things might get a lot worse before they get better. And I won't risk having you two here if that happens."

"Well…how long will we be there? What about you? Are you coming with us? I mean, what about school? What about my friends? This is my last year in middle school. I can't leave now. I have my school dance coming up. And graduation. And—"

"*Michael!*" Her tone was shrill, even on the phone. "None of that stuff matters right now. I have to get you and Nicky out of the country as soon as possible. It's just not safe. You will both be on the next flight out of here whether you like it or not. Now hang tight until your uncle gets there and be ready to move as soon as he arrives. We have no time to waste. Do you understand me?"

"Yes, Mom." I clenched my teeth and squeezed the phone. I forced myself to respond in the most polite way possible so that my mother wouldn't smack me the minute she saw me. But I was furious.

"Okay. I love you. I'll see you soon."

"Love you too. Bye."

I hung up the phone, and my friends stared at me.

"What happened, Michael?" Ashley asked.

"My mom just told me that she is sending my sister and me away. I'm going to New York."

"What? When? For how long?" Tony asked.

"It might be tonight. I don't know for how long. I just know that I'm on the next flight out of here that has room for me and my sister."

"But...why can't you just go home?" Ashley asked.

I shrugged hopelessly. "My mother thinks it's too risky to stay here."

Ashley, Kevin, Tony, and I stared at each other, each at a loss. I was leaving Trinidad and Tobago. I was leaving my home.

"Kevin, grab the phone. Make your call," Danny said, and the moment was gone.

CHAPTER THREE
THE DEPARTURE

"I can't believe my mother would do this to me! How could she just send us away like that?"

"I don't think any of you fully understand how serious this situation is," Danny said. "You heard what the commander of the army said. If anyone is caught outside after curfew, they'll be arrested. The guy on TV seemed crazy enough to enforce something like that. I wish we could all be as fortunate as you right now, Michael. Leaving this country is probably the best thing for everyone to do."

"It still sucks!" Kevin said under his breath.

Kevin was right. I had just turned fourteen. My mustache was starting to come in. And my voice was getting deeper. The girls were finally noticing me. This couldn't happen right now. It would mess everything up. And my friends, most importantly my friends, I didn't want to leave them here. I wanted them to all come with me.

Ashley looked at me. "Honestly, Michael, I kind of agree with Danny. I wish I was getting on a plane with my family too. I don't know how I feel about being a prisoner in my own house. Who does this guy think he is, anyway?"

"I guess you guys are right, it just doesn't make sense right now. You're all not leaving. I still think we could have just gone home and ridden this mess out together. My mom didn't say it was a permanent move though. So hopefully I'll be back in a week or so, after all of this craziness is over."

"Ashley, I think your dad is here." Danny said.

Ashley's dad came barging into the room like he hadn't seen her in months.

"Ashley! Ashley, sweetheart. Where's my daughter?" he shouted at anyone looking in his direction.

"Daddy. Daddy I'm over here!"

He came running across the room, picked her up, and hugged her.

"I'm so glad you're here now, Dad. I've been so scared."

"Don't you worry about anything anymore. Soon we will be home and safe from this mess until everything blows over."

"You think this will all be over soon, Mr. Summers?" Danny asked Ashley's dad. Mr. Summers was a retired cop. If anyone would know, he would.

Mr. Summers sighed. "There are rebel soldiers everywhere. They're patrolling the streets as if they own the place. And they are heavily armed. They're not even wearing masks to hide their identities. I passed by a group of them on the way here and looked right at one of them. I didn't see fear, or concern. All I saw was anger. Our military and law enforcement agencies outnumber them, but for some reason they haven't sprung into action. Something isn't right and no one seems to really know how all of this has happened."

Tony shot me a look. "Woooow! This seems pretty major."

"Yes, Tony. It really is," Mr. Summers replied. "Kevin, Tony, Johnny, your parents asked if I could bring you home since I was coming to get Ashley and I have the truck. Michael, I spoke with your mother and she said your uncle is coming to take you and your sister straight to the airport. I wish we were all so lucky."

"And I wish everyone would stop saying that," I snapped. "I really don't want to go away right now. I want to stay here and be with my friends."

Mr. Summers looked surprised. "Believe me Michael, if this situation gets any worse, you'll be glad you're not here to see it." He looked down at Ashley. "Say goodbye to Michael. We have to get going. I want to make sure I have enough time to get us all home safe and sound."

I gasped. "Goodbye? No, no, no, no, no! This isn't goodbye, Mr. Summers. This isn't goodbye, you guys," I said, looking at Ashley and Kevin desperately. "I'll be back in a week or so. Two, tops. I'm sure this will all blow over and everything will be back to normal before you know it."

"But Michael, what if you end up staying there?" Kevin said.

"That's ridiculous, Kev. We have a house here. My mom has her job. My sister and me are still in school. I don't think we're going to give up all that just because some crazy guy on TV wants to run the country. Trust me. I'll be back home soon, and we can all go back to being friends and hanging out and stuff. Right, Mr. Summers? This is all just temporary, right?"

"I sure hope so, Michael. I really do," Mr. Summers said with a doubtful look on his face.

This was all really happening. Our government was overthrown, my friends were going home, and I was being shipped off to another country.

This was my new reality.

"Hush kids! I think I heard what sounded like a gunshot," Mr. Summers said.

One of the soldiers came running into the office, shouting at the top of his lungs. The room fell silent.

"The rebels are a short distance away and we've just confirmed that they may be headed this way. We need

to get everyone out of here and we have to do it now."

"This is what I feared would happen. We should have left ten minutes ago," Mr. Summers said, grasping Ashley tighter. "Come on, kids. We have to get to my truck."

"But Dad, what about Michael? We can't just leave him here. What if the rebels get to the camp before his uncle does?"

I looked around. There was still a long line of people waiting to use the landline.

"Maybe Michael should go with you, Mr. Summers," Danny suggested. "When his uncle shows up, I'll tell him that he went with you and he can pick him up at your house."

"We have no choice," Mr. Summers said. "Come on, Michael. Everyone to the truck as fast as possible."

Another shot rang out, and then another. The gunshots were getting louder each time—they were getting closer.

"Right over there, kids. The truck is to the left of the parking lot."

Mr. Summers grabbed Ashley by the hand and started running. Kevin, Tony, Johnny, and I took off for the truck behind them. I never thought any of us could run that fast. It was like we had super powers or something.

"Come on, everyone pile in," Mr. Summers said, wrenching open the door. "We're almost out of here."

"Make sure the doors are locked and the windows are all the way up," Mr. Summers said when we were all in. "I'm going to need you all to be very quiet and pay close attention to me until we get home. Now fasten your seatbelts and get ready, this might be a rough ride."

"How are you guys feeling?" I asked, out of breath, as we were pulling up to the gate.

"Relieved, kind of—hey Mike, isn't that your sister and your uncle?" Tony said.

"Where, where?" I replied.

Mr. Summers hit the brake. Everyone jerked forward and Kevin even hit his head on the back of the passenger seat.

"Over there. They're driving into the lot now."

"Oh man! That's them all right," I said.

"Someone get their attention," said Mr. Summers beeping the horn.

"Uncle Dave! Nicky!" I said, rolling down the window. I grabbed my bags, jumped out of the truck, and ran over to Uncle Dave's car.

"Michael. What are you doing out here? You're supposed to be waiting for me inside."

"Ashley's dad was going to take me home because the rebels were getting closer. It was a last minute decision. We had no choice."

"Well I'm glad we made it in time. Come on. Get in the car so we can get out of here. I saw a truck full of rebel soldiers not too far from here."

"Were they coming this way?" Mr. Summers asked my uncle.

"It looked like it." he replied seriously. "Thanks for offering to take Michael with you."

"No problem at all. We should all be on our way now. You guys be safe."

"Michael, get in the car quick," my uncle instructed. "We have to go. They're close."

I glanced back at my friends, wishing I could say a million words with one look. *I'm going to miss you guys. I'll be back soon—I hope.*

I got into my uncle's car and buckled up. Both vehicles then drove off in different directions. I turned round to watch the truck getting smaller and smaller in the distance. It was a horrible feeling not knowing when I would see my friends again…or if I would at all.

"Why are you so upset?" Nicky asked.

"Aren't you?" I replied.

"No. I'm happy to be getting out of here. You should be too. It's not safe here anymore."

My sister and I didn't always agree. And we'd definitely had our fair share of all-out fights. But I knew she always had my back and only wanted what was best for me.

"This is one of those times I wish Dad was around," I said. "He'd know exactly what to do. And I bet we wouldn't be leaving the country."

She scoffed. "You can forget about that because he isn't here. He never is!" She turned around to look at me. "You know it's because of Dad that Mom had to work two jobs until she got her promotion at the airport. Even now, she still cooks food for the office just to make some extra cash. It's why I have to take care of you so often, because Mom's working all the time. All thanks to Dad." The anger was thick in her voice.

I rolled my eyes, wanting nothing more than to punch her.

"Okay you two, that's enough." my uncle said, seemingly oblivious to our hostile conversation. The rest of the ride to the airport went by quietly and felt like hours. I knew my sister was right. But I still wasn't ok hearing it. I sat back and thought about everything that was happening. The past few hours had been like some crazy dream. And now with us leaving, it looked as if it was going to get worse.

"We're here." Uncle Dave's voice broke my chain of thought. Pulling up to the main entrance was like nothing I'd ever seen before. It seemed like everyone was trying to get out of the country. It was a madhouse.

"Thank God!" Nicky muttered.

"How do we even know we're getting on a plane tonight anyway?" I asked.

Uncle Dave turned and looked at me. "I spoke with your mom right before I left to come and get you. She managed to get you both on a flight that leaves in about an hour."

"What? Are you serious?"

"Yes!" Nicky yelled.

I shot Nicky a look. "You can't be that excited about leaving. What about your boyfriend? What about your friends? You won't miss them?"

"Of course I will. But this is like a mini vacation. We are really very lucky to be able to get out of here on such short notice. Now quit complaining and get over it. We're going!"

I looked at her, disgusted. In an even tone, I said, "We may be leaving. But that doesn't mean I have to like it."

"Enough, you two," said Uncle Dave. "Your mother is eager to see you both. Michael, we were able to pack some of your things for you at the house."

Great, probably all of my least favorite clothes, I thought.

"Grab your bags out of the trunk and let's get to your mom's office."

As I got out of the car I heard the last part of a news report that had been playing on the radio.

"The Red House, the prime minister's main headquarters, is ablaze in the capital, Port of Spain—"

Nicky and I looked at each other in disbelief. Uncle Dave took a deep breath and looked down while shaking his head. I guess he was shocked too.

"Let's hurry, kids," he said. "Things are getting really bad really fast. You guys have to get on that plane."

Nicky and I grabbed our bags and headed for my mother's office. It was like a news station in there. Small TVs and radios were on in almost every room. This takeover had everyone's attention. I wondered who was directing the planes, since my mother and the other air traffic controllers all seemed to be watching the news. But then I realized that there were hardly any planes taking off and none were landing.

My mother turned around as we entered the office. "Nicky, Michael! Oh my goodness. I'm so glad to see you both. I've been worried the whole time. Get over here and give me a hug, both of you."

"Ouch, Mom. You're gonna squeeze the life out of me," I said as my mom pulled Nicky and me in for the tightest hug ever.

"Okay, okay!" Mom sighed as she released us. "I'm good now. Let me look at you."

"I'm fine, Mom. Really I am."

"I'm sorry. It's just that everything is so out of control. I couldn't wait to see you both." Mom looked up at Uncle Dave. "Did you hear that they set the Red House on fire?"

"Yup. Heard that just as we were getting out of the car. Lord alone knows what else they're going to do before the night is over."

"And that's exactly why you guys are out of here in the next forty-five minutes. I managed to get you the last seats on the flight."

"But Mom, why do we have to go all the way to New York? Why can't we just stay here, lock the house up, and just stay inside? Uncle Dave, you, Aunt Deb, Shayla, and Alyse can come over. We'll be just fine if we all stay together."

"Michael. That sounds great, but it's not that simple. We're all better off just leaving."

"Well if we're all better off leaving, then how come it's just me and Nicky getting on this plane?"

Mom sighed—the way she did when she was frustrated. "There was only room for the two of you. Plus, I have to stay here for now and take care of some stuff. I'll be in New York with you guys as soon as possible. Don't worry."

"Hey Sue," one of my mom's colleagues began, "the plane is getting ready to board. You should start making your way to the gate with the kids."

My mom looked at us. "Okay guys, this is it. Your aunt Sandy is going to be at the airport in New York to pick you up."

"How long do you think we will be gone, Mom?" I asked, gathering our things.

She looked at me and I saw the fear in her eyes. "I'm not really sure, Michael. We just have to wait and see. I know that it's not ideal for either of you. But it's what's best for the moment. Now come on. We have to get going."

The walk to the gate was not easy for me. All I could think about was how much I wanted to be at home, staying here despite the danger. I had lived in Trinidad and Tobago my entire life. I didn't want to just *leave*.

"Good evening Mrs. B," said the security agent at the gate. "Looks like we're just about ready to go."

Mom turned us around to look at her. "I'm going to need both of you to act your age on this flight. Nicky, you're in charge."

"Of course I am. What else is new?"

"Don't take that tone with me, young lady. You're sixteen years old, which means you're old enough to act like an adult now. Just look after your brother."

I rolled my eyes. "I don't need her to look after me. I've done this flight to New York by myself lots of times."

"Michael, hush! Just listen to your sister and try to behave please. I don't want to hear anything about you guys arguing or anything like that. Got it?"

"Yes, Mom!"

"Now you both know the drill. When you get there and get off the plane, just follow the signs to baggage claim. Then wait for your aunt in the same place we always do. Understand?"

"Yes," Nicky replied.

"Good. Now give me a hug so you can go and sit down."

"You'll be following us soon, right?" I said as my mom pulled me in for another hug.

"Yes. I will."

Mom hugged Nicky.

"I love you both. And I'll miss you until I get there. And don't give your aunt and uncle any trouble please."

"Okay, Mom. We love you too." Nicky said.

As we boarded the plane and looked down the center aisle, it seemed like there wasn't a single empty seat. None of them were assigned. It was first come first served. Nicky and I had to walk all the way to the back before we found two vacant ones.

We fastened our seatbelts. "Okay look," Nicky said, "now that we're alone, just remember that I'm in charge until we get to New York. You have to do what I say."

"Or what?" I sneered.

"Or I'll make this flight very difficult for you," she replied, glaring at me.

"Whatever! I'm going to sleep."

"That's fine with me."

"Just wake me up when they start serving the food."

I turned away from her, towards the window. In a few minutes, we were hurtling down the runway and I watched as my country fell away beneath us. The lights of Piarco International twinkled below us as if nothing was wrong at all. As we flew over Port of Spain fifteen miles to the northwest, I saw the blazing fire that was the Red House.

As we headed to New York City, the cabin lights dimmed, allowing the exhausted passengers an opportunity to sleep. As I stared down into the darkness of the Caribbean Sea below, I could feel the distance between the plane and my home country growing. I refused to believe this was the last time I would see my home, my family, and my friends.

New York would just be temporary.

CHAPTER FOUR
THE ARRIVAL

"Michael, Michael! Wake up. We're going to be landing in about twenty minutes." Nicky gently shook me.

"I'm up," I said, my eyes springing open. "Did we go over the stadium yet? What about the bridges? Did we pass those?"

"No, not yet. We're about to, though."

This was something Nicky and I did every time we flew into New York. We usually arrived at night, so coming into the airport was a spectacular sight since everything was lit up. It was just like in the movies.

"Look, over there. I think that's the stadium," I yelled excitedly. I had woken up optimistic, knowing my visit to New York would be a short one. I might as well enjoy it.

"Yup, that's it. And look over there to the right. That's one of the bridges."

"Wow! That's so cool."

"Ladies and gentlemen, we are beginning our descent and will shortly be arriving at New York's JFK International airport. We ask that you please fasten your seatbelts and remain seated for the duration of the flight. We hope you had a pleasant time flying with us and we do hope you cruise the skies with us again in the near future."

"I guess this won't be so bad. Right Nicky?"

"What do you mean?"

"This could just be another one of our vacations, like you said. Right?"

"You could say so. I don't think we will be here that long," she said.

I nodded, happy. "Okay, cool."

"Ladies and gentlemen, we are cleared for landing and are beginning our descent. Once again, thank you for flying with us. Welcome to New York!"

"I guess this is it," I said. "I hope they put an end to what's happening at home so we can hurry up and get back."

"Me too, Michael. Me too. But let's stop talking about it for now, okay? Let's just relax and have some fun while we're here."

"Okay."

I was starving—Nicky hadn't woken me up when they served dinner. The last time I'd eaten anything was breakfast at camp, more than twelve hours ago.

"I'm so hungry I could eat a cow. You think Aunt Sandy will stop at McDonalds on our way home?

"I hope so. That sandwich they gave us for dinner was terrible."

"Oh yeah? I wouldn't know," I quipped.

After we picked up our suitcases from the luggage carousel, we made our way to arrivals to see if Aunt Sandy was waiting for us. Normally, there was a good chance she wouldn't be. Aunt Sandy was always late. If it were up to her, she would be late to her own funeral.

"Michael, Nicky, over here!" a voice in the distance shouted.

I turned and looked. "Holy smokes! Is that Aunt Sandy? She's actually not late for once."

Nicky followed my gaze. "That *is* her!

We hurried towards her.

"Look how big you both have gotten!" She said as we got close. "Come here and give me a hug. You two must be exhausted. I know it's been a very long and crazy day. I'm just happy your mother got you on a plane before things got worse."

Nicky put her bags down and hugged Aunt Sandy. "Yeah, we're happy too, I guess. But we are definitely tired, and hungry too. Right, Michael?"

I nodded. "Starving!"

"Okay," Aunt Sandy said, turning and picking up Nicky's bags. "Well let's get going. I only paid for an hour of parking. I'm sure we can find somewhere to eat that's open on the way home."

"McDonalds?" I asked excitedly.

She looked back at me and shrugged. "Sure, why not?"

"Perfect!"

We walked through the sliding doors exiting the airport and the wind hit me in the face. "Ahhh yes! Nothing like the smell of that crisp New York air."

"Oh Michael," Aunt Sandy panted, out of breath, moving quickly. "That's nothing but smog and the fumes from airplane engines."

"It must be a good combination then," I said. "It makes me really happy. Relaxed. It brings back good memories of all the times I've been here before."

Aunt Sandy chuckled. "Well if it does that, then take it all in."

We made it to the car with just three minutes to spare, loaded it up, and hit the highway.

"So how are you two feeling?" Aunt Sandy asked, eyeing us in the rear view mirror. I'm sure she had a good idea, but was just trying to keep the conversation light. "You're probably not all that happy about leaving your mother behind, but you must be glad to be here and away from everything that's going on back home?"

Nicky glanced at me and we made eye contact. She was in a much better state of mind to answer that than I was.

"I know I am...him not so much," she answered, jamming a thumb in my direction.

"Really?" Aunt Sandy looked confused. "How come, Michael? I thought you liked coming here to visit?"

I struggled with what to say. How do I tell someone that I've just been forced to leave my home? That I'm not sure I'll ever return? That I wonder if things will ever be normal again for me? "I do," I said. "Everything was just so...sudden. Things went from a normal day at camp to complete chaos in a matter of hours, and now we're in another country." I looked out the window. "But we'll be back home in no time. Right?" I looked forward again having convinced myself that everything would be okay. "I'm really looking forward to finishing the summer with my friends and going back to school for our last year together."

"Well, let's hope so," Aunt Sandy said hesitantly. She didn't look at me in the mirror anymore.

In the back seat, I thought about my predicament. The idea that things could get worse, or even become permanent, crossed my mind after Aunt Sandy made that statement. *What if I never go back home?*

Then the smell of McDonalds fries broke my melancholy. I looked up and there they were—those bright yellow arches, just ahead of us. My mouth began to water in anticipation. I couldn't wait to get my usual: a number two with a large order of fries and a Coke.

Though we were only a few minutes from the house, Nicky and I couldn't wait to eat. We were so hungry we almost inhaled our food. Aunt Sandy had to remind us that we weren't animals and to chew with our mouths closed.

***

"We're here!" Aunt Sandy announced as she pulled into the driveway.

Nicky and I momentarily paused from wolfing down our food to see a completely pitch black house. It was almost midnight. Everyone was surely asleep by now. We had been here many times before; we were about thirty minutes outside of the city, in a middle-class suburban neighborhood. The houses here were all nice and fairly big, with decent sized yards and long driveways. The streets here were lined with huge trees—not palm trees, like home. Everybody on the block knew each other by first name. It was a fun and safe environment to visit. But to live here permanently? I wasn't sure.

"Michael," Aunt Sandy said, unlocking the car doors. "Can you jump out and open the gate for me please?"

"Yeah," I said, wanting to be useful.

As I was lifting the latch on the gate, something glinted through the slightly ajar garage door. I knew exactly what that was. It was Uncle Carl's car. Or should I say his *trophy*. No one could touch that car...or go near it for that matter. It was his prized possession, and he would make sure you knew it too. He'd always talk about it, and wash it in the front of the house for everyone to see. He was always getting compliments about it. Occasionally, very occasionally, he would take me and my cousins Cole and Jake for a ride to the mall, and every time they would make sure he drove down their friends' block so everyone could see us.

I was eager to get inside but all I could think about was the neighbor's giant dog tied up next to the fence separating the two houses. It was the biggest dog I had ever seen, probably at least six feet tall when it stood on its hind legs. I knew what to expect whenever I walked there, but that dog still managed to scare me silly every time.

Aunt Sandy pulled into the driveway. "Uhh, can we go through the front?" I asked closing the gate.

My aunt chuckled. "No, Michael. You know we never use that door except for special occasions. If you're concerned about Butch, don't be. It's late and he's probably sleeping."

"You're such a punk!" Nicky whispered as she walked past me toward the side door.

She had almost reached the door when there was the sound of large chains grazing against concrete. Suddenly, Butch jumped against the wood fence, making it lean. Nicky gasped, flattening herself against the wall of my aunt's house, terrified, then sank to the floor. I couldn't help but burst out laughing. Butch barked wildly.

"Are you okay?" said my aunt helping Nicky up off the ground. Even Aunt Sandy had a small grin on her face.

"Yeah I'm fine," Nicky huffed.

"Who's the punk now, huh?" I commented.

"Shut up, Michael!"

"All right, you two," Aunt Sandy said. "We don't want to wake anyone up. Let's just get inside."

Nicky sighed. "Finally! I'm so glad this day is over." She dropped her bags on the kitchen floor.

"Not just yet, young lady," Aunt Sandy said, wagging her finger. "Let's get these bags upstairs, and then I want both of you to have showers and wash off all that airport crud. Michael, you can use the one down here and Nicky, you use the one upstairs. As soon as you're done, we'll call your mother and let her know you guys have arrived safe and sound. She should be off work by then."

"Yes ma'am," we both said together.

Just then, a deep voice spoke from the living room. "Hey, you two," said Uncle Carl emerging into the kitchen.

"Hey Uncle Carl. I was sure you were sleeping," I said, reaching to shake his hand.

"Hey Michael. Hey Nicky," he replied stretching out his arm.

"I've just been sitting here listening to music for a while. I've also heard about what's been happening down home. Sounds terrible. I really hope they stop that guy."

I sighed, already over the situation. "Me too, Unc. That way we can hurry up and get back home so I can finish the rest of the summer with my friends."

Nicky scoffed. "Oh brother! Will you get over it already?"

I said nothing and gave her the side eye.

"Okay, you two. Hit the showers."

"Roger that Uncle Carl, see you after!"

"Over and out, kids."

Uncle Carl liked the military. Saluting, shaking hands, and using language like that was his thing. Though he had never actually served in the military.

He was definitely the disciplinarian in the house. His presence alone would make you freeze like a deer in headlights. All he had to do was look at you to make you stop whatever you were doing and act right. But deep down, Uncle Carl was cool with me, as long as I didn't cross him. Which trust me, I had no intention of doing so.

Once he grounded Jake for an entire month for trying to climb out of the window and scale down the side of the house. It was something Cole had dared him to do. I think Jake could have done it too. But neither of us expected Uncle Carl to pull into the driveway, right as he was halfway out the window. Jake had hurriedly tried to climb back in once he knew he'd been spotted. But then, to make matters worse, Jake pretended to be asleep when my uncle had come upstairs to find out what was going on. Uncle Carl had woken him up out of his pretend sleep with the loudest shout you had ever heard. He was furious, and more red with anger than I'd ever seen before. Cole and I just stood back and listened to Jake get the longest lecture of his life. By the time Uncle Carl was done his shirt was soaked and his face was dripping with sweat.

But there was a cool side to Uncle Carl, though. He took us to a lot of baseball games, taught us about cars, and he had an awesome knife collection locked away in the basement. Every now and then, we would go down there and listen to him explain about the different types and what they were used for. A few in his collection were old war knives. Between them and the car, Uncle Carl was a pretty cool guy.

"Which room are you taking?" Nicky grunted as we made our way up the steep attic steps. That's where we stayed anytime we came to visit.

"The same one I always take, the one towards the front of the house."

"Why do you always pick that room?"

"Because it's closer to Mom's room," I said, panting, my luggage feeling heavier with each step. "And plus, the sun comes up at the back of the house."

"Whatever! Just help me with the rest of these bags."

We unpacked and had our showers all in under an hour. It was now the middle of the night and time to hit the sack. But Nicky remembered that we had one more thing to do.

"This day just needs to be over! Are you ready to go downstairs?" Nicky had one foot already on the steps. "I want to hurry up and call Mom so I can get to bed."

The words "Let's just call her in the morning" were on my lips, but I paused, realizing I really *should* talk to Mom. I wanted to hear her voice, too. Plus, I wanted to know when she would be getting here.

I nodded. "Let's go."

We silently made our way through the house so we wouldn't wake anyone. Jake and Cole were asleep. As we reached the second floor landing, I heard something unexpected.

"Shhh," I told Nicky, holding my hand up for her to stop. "Do you hear that?"

She kept walking, the stairs creaking under her feet. "Hear what, Michael? I don't hear anything."

"Shhh!" I said again. "Stop walking. It sounds like someone is crying."

Nicky stopped and listened. "Wait. Now I do," she whispered. "It's coming from the living room."

We made our way to ground level and into the living room. On the oversized sofa next to a dim lamp, Aunt Sandy was wiping her eyes. Uncle Carl sat next to her.

"Aunt Sandy, what's wrong?" I asked. "Why are you crying?"

Aunt Sandy opened her mouth to speak then broke down in sobs.

"What's going on?" I asked Uncle Carl.

Uncle Carl said nothing, looking at a loss for words.

I looked back at Aunt Sandy, noticing the house phone in her hands. Her knuckles were white from gripping the receiver.

Aunt Sandy composed herself. "You two," she said, "come sit next to me."

Uncle Carl moved to the other side of the couch, leaving space for me and Nicky to squeeze in. I felt uncomfortable.

The suspense was too much to bear. I looked at Nicky. She had tears in her eyes, as though she knew what had happened.

Aunt Sandy put the phone down and plucked two more tissues from a box on the end table. She dabbed her eyes and took two deep breaths.

"Carl," she croaked. She sounded awful. "Carl, I can't—"

She put her head down and began sobbing again.

Uncle Carl sighed. "Kids," he began.

I had never seen Uncle Carl like this. He had always been strong and stoic. Now...now, he was fragile. It shook me to my core.

"What's happened?" Nicky whispered.

"Your Uncle Dave called while you guys were showering," Uncle Carl said. "The rebels made their way to the airport in an attempt to take control of it."

The airport?

He paused. It seemed as though eons passed.

"Something went wrong and one of the rebels opened fire near your mother's office."

Aunt Sandy's crying grew louder. It was the only sound that filled the room.

Uncle Carl's voice cracked. "I'm so sorry," he said, and a sob escaped him. I inched to the edge of the sofa, my heart pounding in my ears, the urge to scream building up inside of me.

Uncle Carl looked at us. I read the words as they came from his lips.

"A stray bullet hit your mother and...she died."

Suddenly I was very hot, feeling faint and clammy. I couldn't move.

Time stopped.

My breath was moving in and out of me—too slowly, too calmly.

There was a terrible sound in the room, a horrible wailing, that jolted me back to reality. Next to me, Nicky was sobbing, head against Aunt Sandy's chest.

I stared blankly at Uncle Carl. A moment later, I was on my feet, not even realizing I had gotten up. "No! No way!" I was shouting. "This can't be true. We were just with her a few hours ago. Call her. Call Uncle Dave. This isn't real. I want to talk to my mother! I want to talk to my mother now. Give me the ph—"

"*Michael*!" Aunt Sandy interrupted.

Her screaming my name startled me.

"It's true! I'm so sorry. There's nothing we can do right now," she said, her tear filled eyes frightening me. "I know that's not what you want to hear. But we just have to stand by and wait for your Uncle Dave to call us back."

"There's… There's nothing we can do?" I said, gritting my teeth, staring at Aunt Sandy.

I reached for the nearest thing I could get my hands on, a lamp on the coffee table in front of the sofa. I picked it up and threw it across the room.

"Don't tell me there's nothing we can do! My mother is dead. We have to go back home now."

Seeing that I was looking for something else to throw, Uncle Carl lunged toward me, grabbing me and pulling me into his chest.

"Michael," he started. "You have to calm down. There is really nothing we can do from here. Your uncle managed to keep her alive for a short while, but he couldn't get her to the hospital because of the curfew, and she passed away."

The thought of those rebels taking my mom's life infuriated me.

"Did she say anything to Uncle Dave?" I could only imagine what her last thoughts were.

Jagged breaths tore from my throat. My heart felt like it was going to stop. We were going to open a restaurant together. She was going to be around more when we got back home.

"I want to get back home," I mumbled.

I felt Uncle Carl's chest heave. "Not tonight, Michael. Not tonight. Everything in Trinidad is shut down now, including the airport. And we're not sure for how long either."

Realization began to settle in. Nicky and I were going to be here for a while—at least until things got cleared up in Trinidad, maybe even longer.

How could so many horrible things happen in such a short time?

Everything Mom and I talked about in the car on our way to the bus replayed in my mind. Vivid pictures of her laughing when we said that we would only let Nicky work at the front of the restaurant. The thought of when she hugged me right before I got on the bus made my heart begin to race. Then the catalyst—Mom saying she would be here in just a few days. I no longer had that to look forward to.

Sadness washed over me. My knees went weak and they buckled under me. Uncle Carl held on, hugging me even tighter.

Listening to the steady thump of his heart beating made me realize something.

My mother's heart would never beat again.

CHAPTER FIVE
A NEW BEGINNING

Someone tapped me on my shoulder. I groaned, rolling over under the thin blankets.

"Michael. Michael, wake up." It was Nicky whispering softly, shaking my shoulder.

I opened my eyes. "What happened?" I mumbled.

"I feel like I've been hit by a bus," she said. She looked like it too—dark circles under her puffy eyes, her cheeks thin and gaunt. She looked terrible.

"I had the craziest dream," she went on. "I dreamt that…" A look of horror crossed over her face. She realized her nightmare was reality.

My chest felt like a deflated balloon. Everywhere hurt—my body, my mind. I wondered vaguely if I looked as beat-up as Nicky did.

"It really happened," Nicky said, the corners of her mouth turning down. "Mom is gone."

My eyes filled with tears. One of our last moments together came to my mind again. She had dropped me off at the bus for camp, then wrapped her arms around me in a hug, even though I struggled against it in front of my friends. *"One day I'm not going to be around anymore, and you're sure gonna wish you hugged me more often,"* she'd told me.

She'd had no idea how soon that day would come.

My throat constricted and I felt a sob rise up. I swallowed hard, forcing it down.

Don't think about that, Michael, I told myself firmly.

It was a bright sunny day, but everything seemed dark to me. I couldn't feel anything. Honestly, I didn't want to.

The phone rang.

"I'll get it!" We heard Cole's shout from even behind the closed bedroom door.

I pushed all thoughts from my mind and wrenched the bedroom door open, leaving Nicky staring after me in confusion. I couldn't stay in that room, I couldn't.

Aunt Sandy and Uncle Carl were in the dining room with Cole and Jake.

"Mom, it's Uncle Rob. He wants to speak to you." Cole reached out to Aunt Sandy.

I got to the bottom step. "Dad?" I asked. "Pass me the phone!"

Aunt Sandy noticed how purposeful my movements were and handed me the phone. I grasped the receiver and held it up to my ear. Nicky moved close behind me.

"Dad?"

Nicky moved the phone away from my ear slightly so that she could hear what was being said.

"Hey champ! How are you holding up?"

"Champ?" Nicky whispered, rolling her eyes. "He doesn't get to call you that."

"Shhh!" I motioned with my finger on my lips.

"Okay I guess," I said to Dad. "Where are you? When are you coming to get us?"

"I don't know, son. I'm still in London on business. I'm pretty tied up with work and money is kind of tight right now.

I'm not even sure if I'll be able to make it home for your mother's funeral. I'm going to try my best, but everything is up in the air at the moment."

"But after all this mess is taken care of we will be coming back home to live with you, right?"

"I'm not sure, Michael. That's something I'm going to have to think about."

Nicky wrenched the phone from me. "What's there to think about? Either you want us back home or you don't."

I yanked the phone back so we could share it.

"—take that tone with me young lady," Dad was saying. "I'm still your father."

"I don't care! I don't think I want to come home now anyway. I'd rather stay here than live with you."

"That's enough!" Aunt Sandy pulled the phone out of our hands.

I looked at my sister. "Yeah, Nicky. Chill out. Don't you want to go back home?"

She scoffed. "Not if it means living with him. He acts like he doesn't even care."

Aunt Sandy rounded on us. "I said that's enough. You two go and sit in the dining room with everyone else."

She turned to the phone. "Hey Rob."

We were still close enough to hear Aunt Sandy's side of the conversation.

"But I don't understand. They're your children. How can you be so dismissive when it comes to your responsibilities?" she said quietly. "I know you're going through a lot financially and with work right now, and dealing with Sue's

50

passing is going to be very difficult. But this is not going to be easy for Carl and me. We both have full plates of our own with our kids. Now we have two more to look after. Will you at least be able to send us some money to take care of some of the bare necessities until things get sorted out?"

Nicky and I waited.

"Okay then. I guess we don't have much of a choice. We'll touch base next week. Take care."

"Wait!" I said, jumping forward. "Can I say goodbye?"

Aunt Sandy frowned. "Sorry, Michael. He's already hung up." A new look washed over her face. "Carl, can I see you in the kitchen for a few minutes?"

I sat there filled with all sorts of different emotions. I was sad, angry, disappointed, and afraid at the same time. I wasn't sure, but it looked like Nicky was just angry—at least that's all I could see on her face. And I couldn't blame her. Who was this man—who'd said "tied up with work", "funds are tight", and "up in the air"? It's like I didn't even know him, my own father.

"Okay, kids," Aunt Sandy said, emerging from her meeting with Uncle Carl. "We're going to have an impromptu family meeting."

I already had a pretty good idea of what was about to be said. Suddenly the only emotion I felt was anger. If I was correct, I was going to blow a gasket.

"You are all fully aware of the tragedy that took place yesterday," Aunt Sandy started as we gathered around the dinner table. "It's a very sad situation and one we wish never took place. Sue and I were very close..." Aunt Sandy paused, taking a deep breath to avoid crying again. "…But she is gone now. We have to do our best to be strong and move on."

Aunt Sandy looked at Nicky and me.

"Nicky, Michael, I know you both would love to go back home and be with the rest of your family right now, but unfortunately that's not possible. Your father has asked us to take you in for a while until things get sorted out and we've agreed."

Nicky remained silent.

"So basically we are going to be living here now?" I asked sarcastically.

"Yes, Michael. That's correct."

"For how long?" I shot back.

"We're not really sure, for a few months at least."

I looked Nicky square in the face. She seemed bewildered, like a deer in the headlights.

"I guess you got your wish," I spat.

I threw my chair from under me and stormed out of the room. I needed to get some fresh air.

This was too much. My life had gone from normal to completely crazy in less than a day.

***

Why is this happening to me? Why now? What did I do to deserve this?

"Hey kid!" Uncle Carl said chasing me out onto the front stoop, interrupting my thoughts.

"Hey," I muttered.

He sat down with a groan. "I know this is a lot for you to take in right now. But you have to know that you aren't alone in this. We are all hurting and we are all affected by this terrible situation. We all loved your mother dearly and we'll miss her. But she's in a better place now. Your aunt and I are going to do everything we can to take good care of you and your sister. It might be tough at times, but we'll be there for you. I'll be there for you."

I sighed. I didn't really want to hear the "let's move on" speech right now. It was way to soon for that. Couldn't I have a moment without being pulled in a hundred directions? "I just wish that things didn't have to be this way."

"We all do, Mike. But sometimes things happen that we have no control over."

No control over? My mind raged. But this was a battle I didn't want to fight—not now.

"I guess," I mumbled.

The front door opened. Cole stuck his head out.

"Can we sit with you guys?" he asked.

"Sure son! Actually, I was just leaving." Carl groaned again as he pushed himself off the step.

Cole and Jake sat next to me. Cole wrapped his arm around my shoulders. I tensed up.

"Living with us won't be so bad," Cole said. We'll do lots of fun stuff together."

"And we go out to a new restaurant to eat every week. You'll like living here," Jake added.

I wanted to believe him, I really did. But I couldn't just yet. It was still too fresh.

"Yeah. I guess. We'll see.

"Wanna know what the best part is?" Cole asked, excitedly.

"Yeah?" I asked wearily. "What's that?"

"Going back to school."

I grunted. "How is that the best part?"

"Because we get to go shopping for all new stuff. New clothes, new sneakers, new book bags, new everything."

That was a new concept to me. We wore uniforms back home so we never really had to worry about getting new clothes. But getting new clothes wouldn't be enough of a distraction, though. Nicky and I were stuck here. Mom was dead; Dad was across the ocean, far away. New clothes couldn't fix that.

"I guess that might be cool," I said. I was too exhausted to say anything else.

"Trust me, it is," Jake said. "Mom makes it an all day event. We go to the outlets and just rack everything up. School starts in a couple of weeks so we should be going soon."

I scoffed, remembering all over again how helpless I was, as another thought came to me. "Hopefully my dad sends some money so that I can get some new stuff too."

"We're family now, Mike," Cole said. "I'm sure Mom and Dad will take care of you, even if he doesn't, so that you can be ready for when you start your new school. And you can always borrow some of my stuff from last year since we're about the same size."

The thought of starting a new school and becoming part of a new culture scared me. I couldn't begin to imagine what to expect. I was popular back home. Even with the teachers—I could get away with almost anything. I had been doing really well in all of my classes. This year was going to be a light load for me. And the dance! I was all set to ask Kimberly to the dance. I was sure she would have said yes.

What would my life be like at the new school?

The front door opened slightly. "Hey guys, come inside and get washed up," Aunt Sandy said. "I'll make you breakfast."

I heaved myself up off the step. I felt as old as Uncle Carl—running on empty, exhausted. After all, I had only just woken up.

Nicky was waiting for me inside.

"I'm sorry if what I said on the phone to Dad upset you even more," she said. "Now is definitely no time for us to be mad at each other."

I looked at her blankly. I wasn't expecting that. In fact, I didn't even care about what she had said. But she was right. I needed her for support—and she needed me.

"Apology accepted, sis," I said.

She offered a melancholy smile. "Love you kid!"

"Love you back, sis."

She was all I had left.

CHAPTER SIX
SCHOOL

The blaring of my alarm clock startled me out of my sleep. It was 5:15 on Monday morning and this was my first day at my new school. My stomach churned—I was nervous.

Two weeks had passed like it had been two days. I hadn't really talked much or done anything since Mom died. I'd been keeping to myself, thinking about this new life that Nicky and I had been forced into. Naturally, there'd been a sense of heaviness around the house. Nicky said it was normal to feel down for a while. "It's part of the grieving process," she told me. If it were up to me I'd stay in bed all day eating cereal and watching TV. But that wouldn't help. I had to get myself together and try to make the best of this new chapter of my life. I just hated that it was without Mom.

As my feet hit the cool hardwood floor, a tingling sensation went up through my body all the way to my head. I sat up straight, took a deep breath, and stretched.

I glanced over at the chair next to my bed where my clothes were laid out. Funds were tight for Aunt Sandy and Uncle Carl, so I had been given some of Cole's hand-me-downs. Turns out Uncle Carl and Aunt Sandy didn't have any extra money for me to get some things for school. Nicky just needed clothes. We just had to wait and hope Dad would send some money. I sighed. I knew how important it was to look good at school, especially on the first day. And just like that, the only thing I wanted to do was go back to sleep.

"Michael. Are you up?" Aunt Sandy yelled up the stairs. "We're leaving in the next thirty minutes. So put some pep in your step!"

I dragged myself off the bed and shuffled to the bathroom.

"Aw man! Where did this pimple come from?" I murmured, looking in the mirror.

Just another thing to worry about.

I wasn't hungry, so I just brushed my teeth, used the toilet, and went back to my room. I mustered up enough enthusiasm to start getting ready even though it was the last thing I wanted to do. My palms were already sweating and my heart was racing. *Nervous* wouldn't begin to describe how I was feeling. *Terrified* would be more appropriate.

A knock at the door. "Are you decent?" Nicky asked.

I was still in my pajamas. "You can come in."

Nicky opened the door and looked at me. "You're not ready yet?"

"For what? To look stupid and be the object of everyone's ridicule?"

Nicky rolled her eyes. "I really don't think it's going to be that bad."

"To you it might not be. You're not going to a new school where no one knows who you are. Look how long it took me to become popular in school back home. I worked hard for that. And now I have to start all over again."

She waved her hand, like that would solve everything. "Don't worry about that. Just be yourself. You'll make new friends in no time and everything will be fine."

She clearly had no idea.

"Whatever," I mumbled. "I just hope no one says anything about this shirt." I held it up. "Can you tell it's old?"

"Now I can," Nicky said, chuckling.

"That's not funny. This is one of the best shirts I could borrow from Cole. It's from last year. I can't wait 'til we can go shopping for myself. This is so embarrassing."

"Oh relax. I'm sure you won't be the only one wearing something from last year. "

"Let's hope so!" I looked at her seriously, pleading. "Why can't we just go back home? Why won't Dad just come and get us? Does he really not want us or something?"

Nicky sighed and sat next to me on the bed. "I don't really have an answer for that. But for now, you're going to have to get over the idea of going back home, Michael. This is our new home. We're going to be here for a while at least, so we just have to make the best of it." Her eyes searched mine, waiting for a response. She realized I had none to offer. "Now hurry up and get downstairs before you get left behind."

"That wouldn't be the worst thing," I mumbled.

Nicky had a firmness about her. Like nothing fazed her. But I knew deep down, she was dealing with Mom being gone in her own way. She never liked to show weakness. I guess she always felt like she had to be strong in front of me. After all, she practically had a hand in raising me. Maybe she thought that the only way I would listen to her was if she was strong.

She stood up and left my room. Watching her deal with her grief so much more easily while I continued to wallow seemed as hard as actually living here now.

***

"What's up Mike?" Cole greeted me as I got to his bedroom door. "I can't decide which one of my new shirts to wear, and which pair of sneakers. Looking good takes so much work. I'm excited though. Are you excited?"

I thought my sour emotions were displayed pretty well through my frown.

"Do I look excited?" I snarled.

"Wow! Take it easy cuz!" He put his hands up in mock surrender.

"Sorry man. I'll meet you in the car."

I was starting to feel really annoyed already.

"Morning, Michael." Aunt Sandy was sounding chipper. I wasn't sure if it was the coffee or the fact that she still had one more week of vacation time.

"Good morning."

"How are you feeling?" she asked.

There was no point in telling the truth. *It's time to start looking ahead, Michael*, they'd say to me again. *This is your life now.*

Aunt Sandy was looking at me expectantly.

"Great!" I said.

"Ready for your first day?"

"Yup!" I rolled my eyes behind her back. One-word answers were my way of avoiding how I really felt.

"Here's some breakfast to go, and some money for lunch." She pressed a five-dollar bill into my hand. Awesome, I could get a nice meal with five bucks. "It's not a lot but it should hold you over until Friday." My heart dropped. Five dollars for the whole week? How would I make that last? "Hopefully your father sends some money for you and your sister by then too."

"If he does, can we please go shopping for some new clothes?"

"We'll have to see how much, if anything, he sends first. Then we can talk about that."

I sighed. I couldn't get angry with Aunt Sandy and Uncle Carl—I knew they were doing the best they could, what with having the responsibilities and cost of two additional children thrust upon them.

"I'll go wait outside."

Jake was already in the car. He was always the first one because he wanted to make sure he got the front seat.

"What's up?" he said, chomping down on his breakfast sandwich.

"Nothing," I sighed. "Ready to get this day over with already."

The smell of bacon and eggs filled the car as Cole and Aunt Sandy hastily made their way inside. We definitely couldn't be late for the first day. I shoved my breakfast sandwich in my bag. Maybe that would be my lunch.

"Okay, let's get you guys to school," Aunt Sandy said, reversing out of the driveway.

We had a thirty-minute drive ahead of us. Cole and Jake's school was the first stop. My new school was ten minutes further.

I stared out of the window in silence taking in the scenery, hoping that it would take my mind off things. It didn't. My stomach was in knots.

"I can't wait to see all the new girls this year," Cole said. "I hope I get best dressed again. This year is gonna be perfect"

I tried to ignore Cole, but to no avail. He wouldn't stop talking about his fancy clothes, his new sneakers, and seeing all of his friends again. He and Jake were popular at their school. But Jake wasn't really into all the flashy stuff. He was more laid back, kind of quiet actually. You never really knew what was going on in his head.

Aunt Sandy glanced in the rear view mirror and saw how upset I was. Sensing my discomfort, she changed the subject.

"Cole, are you going to be on the debate team again, or will you sit this year out and try something new?"

"I don't know. Haven't really thought about it."

Aunt Sandy turned a corner. The school was just ahead. "Do we have to go over the rules again?"

"No Ma! We're good on the rules." Jake said.

"Yup, we're good," Cole echoed.

"Say it anyway," Aunt Sandy demanded.

Cole and Jake rolled their eyes. "No fighting, no cursing, no inappropriate behavior, be respectful, and make sure we're home by 5:00."

"Perfect!"

"Can we jump out right here, Mom? This is our last year. We should be taking the bus to school like all the other kids," Cole said.

"Are you guys embarrassed by me?"

I glanced at Jake and Cole. They had no idea how lucky they were, to have their mom drive them to school...*to have their mom at all.*

"No Mom. It's not that. It's just—"

"It's fine," Aunt Sandy interrupted. "You guys can all start taking the bus next week."

"Cool! See ya!"

"Later Mike!" Cole and Jake said, scurrying out of the car.

I couldn't believe how big their school was. It looked like an old castle, with pillars on each side of the front door, statues on each corner of the front wall, and vines covering the whole front. They must have been growing for years.

"Your school is just a few blocks away, Michael," Aunt Sandy said pulling away form the curb. "About another ten-minute drive."

"Great! Another ten minutes of angst." I said under my breath as we started away.

"Since you're transferring, I'm going to walk you in and drop off all of the paperwork. Then someone else will take it from there. Okay?"

"Okay."

"Do you have anything you want to ask me before we get there?"

"Not really," I said, lying of course.

I did have questions. A lot. But I couldn't ask Aunt Sandy. She wouldn't understand what I was thinking or how I was feeling. I needed a guy for this kind of thing. *Maybe I'll talk to Uncle Carl when I get home.*

Are you sure? Because you can ask me anything. If I don't have an answer for you right away I'll do my best to have one for you by the time you get home.

I thought for a few seconds. Maybe I could talk to her. *Nah!*

"I'm sure. Thanks though."

"Okay. Well if you do, let me know."

"I will" *Unlikely!*

The rest of the journey went by quickly and it wasn't long until we arrived outside the school.

"Ah! Someone's coming out of a spot. Lucky break. Parking here is never easy. And it looks like we made it in less than ten minutes," she said waiting for the other car to leave before pulling into the parking space.

I grabbed my book bag out of the trunk and Aunt Sandy locked the car. With every step we took toward the front entrance, I could feel my heart race faster. This school was huge, much newer and cleaner looking than Cole and Jake's. A statue of the team mascot—a patriot—held up the school flag. A dozen thoughts ricocheted around my mind about whether or not I'd make friends, if I would be accepted, be made fun of, or whether anyone would notice this mountain of a pimple on my face.

We were suddenly at the front desk.

"Good morning," Aunt Sandy greeted the receptionist. "My name is Sandy Peters and this is my nephew Michael Bell. He's transferring here today."

"Good morning ma'am. Okay. Do you have the paperwork we mailed to you?"

"Yes I do."

"Great. You can have a seat. I'll let someone in the principal's office know that you are here."

"Thank you."

Aunt Sandy and I sat next to each other.

"This is your last chance to ask me any questions," she pressed.

"Questions like what?"

"Anything!"

"I don't have any."

"Well let me say a few things to you." The chair squeaked as she turned to face me. "I know that this isn't the best situation right now. But you have to believe that your uncle and I are going to do everything we can to make this transition as smooth as possible for you and your sister. We love you both like our own children and we are here for you. Now, school here is very different than back home. You don't have as much freedom and you certainly have way more rules. Respect your teachers and anyone in authority for that matter. Make sure you focus in class and ask questions if you have to. Choose your friends wisely. If they curse, sag their pants, are disrespectful to teachers and other students, or if they have any kind of gang affiliation, you should not be friends with them.

As a matter of fact, stay as far away from anyone who fits that description."

"How will I know if they're in a gang?"

"Gang members usually have something on them which shows which one they're in. It could be something in a particular color, a cap, a tattoo, or even something as simple as a wristband."

"Oh, okay." I wasn't into any of that stuff.

"Lastly, be yourself. Remember that you are unique and you are cool just the way you are. Don't try to change for anyone or anything. Got it?"

"Got it." I replied.

A tall lady in a black dress with glasses and a full head of gray hair emerged from a back office. "Mrs. Peters, and Michael, is it?"

"Yes," Aunt Sandy said, shaking the woman's hand.

"My name is Mrs. Green. I'm the principal here."

"It's a pleasure to meet you. I didn't think we would be seeing you, though."

"I like to meet all of my new students on their first day, walk them to their homeroom class and make them feel a little more at ease."

"Great. Well, I guess I'll head off now then. Is everything okay with his paperwork?"

"Yes. We're all set."

"Ok, I'll be back to pick you up this afternoon, Michael."

I smiled, willing myself to be more positive. *Make the best out of a bad situation*, I told myself.

"Let's get you to your first class. We only have a few minutes until the bell rings."

Everyone kept saying hi to Mrs. Green as we walked through the halls. She seemed cool. She had a nice smile and seemed approachable. But there was also a sternness about her. She was poised; intentional about the way she used her words. And when she spoke to you, she looked you straight in the eye. It was quite unnerving.

Walking through the halls was like walking through a museum. Everything was immaculate and seemed bigger somehow. The walls were covered with what looked like paintings done by the students. And there were shelves built in to the walls that held dozens of trophies from the school's athletic teams.

"You guys have a swim team here?" I asked as we walked by a collection of swimming trophies.

"Yes we do. We also have a basketball, football, tennis, and volleyball team. Were you on the swim team in Trinidad?"

"How do you know that's where I'm from?"

"It's in your paperwork."

Duh. Get with the program, Michael. "Yes. I was one of the best in my school. I have a lot of trophies and medals myself back home. I'll probably never see that stuff again though." I sighed.

"I also read that your mother has recently passed away. I am so sorry. I know what it feels like. My mother passed away a few months ago."

"But I'm sure she was much older."

"Yes. I am sure she was," Mrs. Green said. "But it still hurts not having her around. I know this will be a difficult time for you. And I want you to know that you can come to my office anytime and for anything."

"Thank you."

"You're welcome." She stopped in front of a classroom door. "Here we are!"

As we entered the classroom I took a deep breath, stuck my chest out, and tried my best to display some confidence. Mrs. Green stood at the front of the class, and I stood awkwardly behind her.

The bell rang.

"Everyone, settle down. Mrs. Green has an announcement she would like to make," the homeroom teacher said. The placard on her desk read *Miss Rose*.

"Good morning class."

"Good morning, Mrs. Green," the class replied in unison, the way all classes do.

"I would like everyone to meet Michael." She grasped my shoulders as if she was presenting me as the class' newest specimen. "He is from Trinidad and will be joining us for the rest of this school year. I expect you all to give him a warm welcome and make him feel at home."

"Yes Mrs. Green," the class said resoundingly.

Mrs. Green smiled at me and then turned to Miss Rose. "Okay, Miss Rose. He's all yours. Remember Michael, anytime and for anything."

"Yes ma'am."

"What's your last name, Michael?" Miss Rose asked, looking in her attendance book.

"Bell."

"Okay. You're going to be sitting right over there." She pointed. "First row to the right."

"In the front?" I gasped.

I was sure I was going to get to pick my own seat. Just like back home.

"Yes. Right up front."

There was a second bell, prompting some last-minute stragglers bolting into the room, all of whom Miss Rose knew by first name. I was the only new kid in class.

Ten minutes passed while Miss Rose took attendance and went over her rules. Then she asked us to share a little bit about what everyone did over the summer.

"Michael, we've heard from some of the other kids. But you are the only new student. Why don't you tell us a little bit about yourself?"

I was caught off guard and didn't know where to start. *Do I tell them about all the normal stuff like hanging out with Kevin and the rest of the gang, playing soccer, and riding around the neighborhood and stuff? Or do I tell them about all of the action that took place during camp, all the guns I saw and army trucks that shook the building? Do I tell them about Mom?*

"Michael?"

"Yes. Sorry Miss Rose. My name is Michael...I'm from a small country in the West Indies, in the Caribbean, called Trinidad and Tobago. My summer was pretty regular. I just went to the same camp I've been going to for the past few years."

"What are some things you like to do?" Miss Rose continued.

"I'm a strong swimmer. I'm into other sports like soccer and tennis. But I really like to cook."

"Well that's very good, Michael. We are glad to have you with us."

"Where did you get that shirt? It looks kinda dingy," someone said from the back.

A few of the other students began to laugh out loud.

"*Vince!*" Miss Rose said sternly.

"And is that how everyone talks where you're from? If so, you might want to pay extra close attention in English class," said Vince again.

More laughter.

"Vincent! That's enough."

I looked back to see who Vince was. How stupid can someone be? My English was just fine. *Do I sound that bad? Do I need to learn to speak with an American accent? How long will that even take?*

Vince looked older than me, already sporting a full mustache. He was much bigger too, like he could be on the wrestling team. All his clothes were brand spanking new. His orange shirt and black jeans matched the color of his sneakers. To top it all off, he also had a nice-sized gold chain. *Who has a gold chain in the eighth grade?*

Vince caught me looking at him and locked eyes with me. All I saw was aggression. He had a menacing look to him, kind of like the expression I saw on the commander of the rebels back home. Vince also had a four-inch scar across his left cheek. Something like that could only come from a bad fight. He sat in the middle of two other guys who looked just as old as he did. My guess was that they'd all been left back at least once. Even still, I bet they got all the girls and everyone wanted to hang with them. Being part of that crew would be cool I thought.

"Stop looking back there like that," the kid at the desk next to me said. "Vince and the rest of his crew are pretty reckless. They look for any reason to get into fights and start trouble all the time. And the way you're looking back there is reason enough."

I faced forward again and looked at the kid next to me.

"Who are you?"

"My name's Andrew. I was a transfer student in this class last year. So I know all about how this goes."

"Oh." I replied, trying to let Vince's comments roll off my shoulders. "Well I wasn't trying to start anything. Where are you from?"

"I'm from the Caribbean like you. Jamaica to be exact."

"That's cool. Some of my friends back home were from Jamaica."

The bell rang. It was time to go to first period.

"Where do we go now?"

"We have science class now. We all move as a group throughout the day. You can walk with me."

For the first time since being here, I felt a sense of relief. "Cool!"

As we walked through the halls, though, I felt strange. I was used to having my friends beside me. Now, with only one person next to me, the feeling of isolation consumed me. I was the new kid on the block. No one knew my name. I didn't have the respect of anyone in this school. And I sure didn't have the attention of any of the girls. I'd have to get to work on building a name for myself here…and quickly.

CHAPTER SEVEN
COUNSELING

"Knock knock!" said a lady, sticking her head into the classroom.

"Good morning, Miss Smith. Picking someone up?" Mr. Jimenez asked.

"Yes, actually. Michael Bell."

My heart immediately started pounding. This was not how I wanted to start my day. *Who the heck was Miss Smith?* I thought, looking toward the door. *And what does she want with me?* It had been three weeks at the new school and I hadn't seen her once.

"Right over there." Mr. Jimenez said, pointing my way.

"Come with me, Michael," Miss Smith said, motioning into the hall.

The other kids were looking at me strangely. It was as if they knew something I didn't.

"Who are you?" I asked as the classroom door closed behind me.

"My name is Miss Smith. I'm one of the guidance counselors here and your name came up on my list."

"Counselor? I don't need to see a counselor. Who put me on that list?"

"Your name may have only come up because you're a new student here. That happens a lot."

"Oh, okay," I said, breathing a sigh of relief. "Because I'm fine."

If this lady only knew how much of a lie that was, she would set up appointments with me for the rest of the year. These past few weeks had been agonizing, It constantly felt like someone was looking down at me because of my worn out, borrowed clothes, for not having any friends, and trying to think of how to make a name for myself. Because Dad still hadn't sent any money for Nicky and me. And Mom...I really missed Mom. I tried to block that out, though. I had to. It was the only way I wouldn't fall apart in this place.

But there was no way I could let Miss Smith know any of this.

"Right this way, Michael. My office is at the end of the hall."

"Okay."

Miss Smith's office was huge and smelled of fresh flowers. All of the windows were open and the walls were painted a bright yellow. I don't know how she got any work done in here. All I could think of was taking a nap. I felt extremely relaxed.

"Have a seat on the couch," she said, pointing to the other side of the room.

I was apprehensive. My palms were clammy and little beads of sweat were already forming on my forehead. What were we going to discuss? What would she ask me? What would I say?

"So, how are you?" she asked, rolling her chair closer to the couch I was sitting on.

"I'm great! How are you?" I said as confidently as possible. I had to stay cool.

"I'm well, thank you. I want you to know that right now we are only meeting because it's just how we do things at this school. Over the next few weeks I will be checking on you, just to see how things are going. But, as the eighth grade counselor, I am available to you any time you feel like you need to talk. All you have to do is stop by my office."

"But why? Don't you have other kids with more important stuff going on that you need to talk to?"

She nodded. "Yes I do. But I want to be available to you as well."

"I probably won't need to," I said. "But okay."

"So tell me a little about yourself."

Here we go. Couldn't I just go through school without anyone knowing anything about me? I didn't want to be disrespectful though, so I took a deep breath and thought about the most basic information I could.

"I'm Michael Bell. I'm thirteen years old. I'm from Trinidad. I like soccer and swimming, and I have an older sister."

There! I thought to myself. *Now you know me.*

"That's great. Can you tell me some more? Perhaps about the school you transferring from? What made your family move to New York?"

My stomach was beginning to turn. Memories of leaving camp, barely making it out alive, the feeling of sadness I'd felt leaving my home and my friends, getting on that plane not knowing when I'd return, and Mom—finding out what happened to her at the airport...all of this rushed through my head. I'd been avoiding them like the plague. And I wasn't about to go there now.

"If it's okay with you, I'd rather not talk about that today," I said, feeling my heart speed up.

"Okay. That's fine with me. Do you think we can talk about it another time?" Miss Smith asked while writing something down on her notepad.

"What are you writing down?" I sat up on the couch.

"Just some notes. So how about it? Can we talk about it another time?"

"Maybe."

"Okay. You let me know when you are ready."

"I will."

I was surprised she let me off that easily. Maybe this counseling stuff wouldn't be so bad if she was a nice lady.

The bell saved me from going any further. I was ready to get out of there and get to my next class.

"Well there's the bell. I just wanted to get acquainted with you for a few minutes. The next time we meet will be for a full period," said Miss Smith.

"Ok," I replied.

***

Math class hadn't begun yet, so everyone was talking softly among themselves.

"So what's wrong with you?" a voice said loudly. It was Vince. I turned and looked at him. He was staring right at me.

"What do you mean?" I asked.

"Are you depressed? Do you have anger issues or something? Are you on drugs? What is it? If you're seeing Miss Smith, something has to be wrong with you."

The room went quiet. So quiet I could hear Andrew breathing from about five feet away. All eyes were on me. It was as if everyone wanted me to confess to some kind of mental illness or past trauma that required me to get help. My defenses began to spring up.

"There's nothing wrong with me," I spat. "It's just because I'm a new student here."

"That's what she told you?" Vince said, chuckling. A few of the other students did the same.

"That's all it is!" I insisted.

Suddenly, the classroom door swung open as the teacher walked in. "Good morning class. Settle down. The late bell will ring in a few seconds so let's get our textbooks out and open them to lesson number five."

Mr. Lee was right on time. I didn't know where that conversation with Vince had been going. But I'd needed it to end right then.

"Is there really something wrong with you?" Andrew asked softly, leaning over to me.

"No! I'm fine," I snapped back at him.

No one could know how I really felt. I simply wanted to disappear.

Math was one of my favorite subjects so this would be a good distraction. But before we could really get into the lesson, the period was over.

"I hope you're not letting Vince get to you," said a girl behind me as we left the classroom.

"What do you mean?" I said turning around to see who had spoken.

"He can be a real jerk sometimes. Always talking trash. Always picking on people. That's why we broke up. My name is Sarah by the way."

"You used to date Vince?" I asked surprised.

Sarah was the best-looking girl I'd seen in the school so far. And she seemed smart too. *I wonder why she'd gone out with him in the first place?*

"He wasn't always like that. But ever since his fath—"

"Hey Sarah, come on!" A girl called Jill yelled from down the hall. She was cute too, but not as attractive as Sarah.

"Sorry, gotta go."

"Wait, what were you going to say?"

"Don't worry about it. See you later, Michael." She smiled, then turned and ran toward Jill.

"Shoot. I wonder what it was," I muttered to myself.

"You okay, Mike? Are you talking to yourself?" Andrew asked, walking toward me.

"I'm good."

"Let's get down to the lunchroom. It's pizza day and I'm starving." Andrew said, holding his belly.

"Me too,"

"Let's hurry so we can get to table one. I hate when there's only the plain cheese slices left."

We both sped up so that we would have first dibs on the best slices.

"I want to tell you something," Andrew said, out of breath by the time we reached the cafeteria.

"What is it?"

"I used to see Miss Smith at least twice a week."

"Really? For what?"

"When my family moved here from Jamaica, things were really hard for us. We didn't have much and I went through a lot in my first few months here."

I looked at him, my mind far away from pizza now. "What kind of things did you go through?"

"I was bullied a lot. The other kids made fun of me because of my accent, my clothes, and they even made fun of my parents when they came to pick me up from school."

"How did you deal with it?" I asked.

"At first I didn't know how to, but Miss Smith really helped me. My father did too. He told me to just focus on my schoolwork and to let my grades do the talking. He's a doctor. And my mother is a college professor. We're doing a lot better now since we first moved here. I see the way you look when Vince talks to you and I know exactly how you feel. Talking to Miss Smith might not be so bad."

I bristled. "What makes you think I don't want to talk to her?"

Andrew laughed. "No one does. You only see her when you have 'issues.'" He did air quotes around the word. "And no one wants to be labeled."

Turning away, I said, "Well I really don't have anything to talk to her about anyway. But thanks for letting me know."

"Everyone has something they need to talk about. We all go through stuff. I'm sure you do too, right?"

I turned and glared at him. "No nothing! Now let's drop this."

Andrew's eyebrows rose. "A little defensive are we?"

"Defensive? I don't know what you mean? I'm not being defensive. I just don't want to talk about it."

He chuckled. "Saying you're not being defensive usually means that you are."

"Let's just stop talking about it okay?"

He put his hands up in surrender. "Okay, okay. I'll stop. I was just trying to help."

"Well I don't need help. I just need you to be my friend."

"Okay."

"Okay."

"Are we good?" Andrew said with his hand out."

"We're good." We shook on it and then headed to table one where our classmate Matt was already sitting.

"Where have you guys been? They're about to call us up," said Matt.

"Chill out, Matt. We're here now." Andrew said trying to ease his seemingly anxious mood.

I usually spent most of my time with Matt and Andrew. They were the two kids in my class that I felt most relaxed around.

A voice came over the cafeteria loudspeaker. It was Mr. Haber, one of the assistant principals.

"Will table one please form a line to be served. Table one, please form a line."

"Let's go, guys," I motioned to Matt and Andrew.

Andrew led the way, followed by Matt, then me. Even though we were at table one, we had to pass all the other tables to get to the food. Matt slowed as we got closer to table six, where Vince and his crew were sitting.

"What's up Vince?" he said, giving him a fist bump.

"What's up Matt? Why don't you come sit with us? We have plenty of room," Vince asked.

"No thanks man. I'll stay where I am."

"Okay. Your loss, bro! Come back whenever you're ready."

"Come back? What does he mean come back?" I hissed, tapping Andrew on his shoulder.

Andrew turned around, just as confused as I was.

"Let's go, you three. You're holding up the line," a teacher said from behind us.

Matt got back into the line and we continued walking. We all got our food and headed back to the table. I was eager to ask Matt about his exchange with Vince.

"So how do you know Vince?"

Matt's body tensed up a bit. He gave me a look like he didn't want to talk about it. But I had to know. "Well?"

"We grew up in the same apartment building and went to elementary school together," he said after a few seconds.

"Oh okay." I let some time go by. "What did he mean when he said you could come back whenever you're ready?"

He laughed it off and turned away. "Oh, nothing!"

"What do you mean 'nothing'? Was it like…you can come back to the table? Or you can come back to the group? What was it?"

"It's nothing, Mike!" he whispered. "You should drop it."

I looked over at Andrew; but he just put his head down and avoided me.

"All right! Sorry I asked."

I turned to look down the rows at table six. Vince's table was definitely the cool table, home to the school's most popular kids. Anyone sitting there would automatically earn rank at school. Plus, Sarah was sitting there. If I'd gotten an invitation to sit with them, I would have been all over it. I couldn't help wonder why Matt had decided not to.

The bell was about to ring and Mr. Haber started telling everyone to throw out our trays. When table one was called we all walked up to the trash together. On our way back, Andrew went to grab another piece of fruit. I thought Matt was right next to me but when I looked he wasn't there.

"Where's Matt?" Andrew asked as he got back to the table.

"I've no idea! He just vanished."

"Guess we'll catch up with him next period."

"Guess so."

We were headed to English.

"Pssst! Over here!" It was Matt. He was calling to us from the doorway of one of the teachers' bathrooms.

"What are you doing in there? And how did you even get in?"

"Relax. No one ever uses this bathroom. I just jimmied the lock. Come on, get in here," he said as he ushered us inside and shut the door.

"So what's going on? Why have you got us in here?" I asked hastily. If we got caught, we'd be in big trouble.

"I couldn't tell you at lunch because no one knows about it. Well, except for Andrew."

"I knew it," I hissed. "That's why you were avoiding me."

"I couldn't say anything either," Andrew said.

"Well what is it then? Were you a part of his crew or something?"

"I was. But not for long, just a week. It was too much for me and I had to get out."

"Only one week? What happened?"

"I told you before that me and Vince grew up together, right. We were always cool and always had each other's backs. But as we got older, he changed, and started to get a little crazy."

"Why? Did something happen?"

"Vince's father was the leader of one of the biggest gangs in Queens. Everyone knew him, and everyone feared him too. Then one day, when we were in sixth grade, a drug deal went really bad and Vince's father got busted. A rival gang got to him in prison and they beat him to death. Vince has been angry and messed up ever since."

So that's what Sarah was about to tell me.

My eyes widened. "Wow! That's crazy. But what does that have to do with you?"

"The gang broke up shortly after Vince's father died. But Vince wanted to have a small gang of his own in memory of his dad. He asked me to join him. So his brother, me, and a few others did."

"What happened?"

"We attacked another crew the same week I joined. The only problem was that we didn't have weapons and they did."

Matt lifted his shirt and showed me a massive scar on the left side of his stomach. Then he turned and showed me several other small scars on his back.

"What the heck happened to you?" I asked, appalled.

"I got stabbed twelve times in that fight."

I was fixated on those scars. I couldn't say a word. Matt could easily have died.

"And that's why you left?" Andrew said.

Matt nodded. "I was in hospital for three weeks and out of school for almost a year. Anyway, those guys are bad news. Vince will always be a friend...but only from a distance."

"Mike!" Matt said, snapping me out of my stupor.

"Yeah. What's up?"

"I saw how you were looking over at table six today. You want to sit at that table?"

"No way bro. Why would you say that?"

He glared at me. "Because it's the same way I used to look at them when I left the gang. A part of me wanted to go back and be with them. But it's just not an option for me."

"I mean, it would be cool to be part of the popular group. Maybe a bit of me does want to hang with them. What's so wrong with that?" I said.

"After the way he's made fun of you and talked trash about you? You would still want to be his friend? Are you crazy?" Andrew said, alarmed.

"I'm not saying I want to be friends with them like that. Just to be seen with them and getting to know them would be pretty cool.

Matt shook his head. "To get to know them is to be friends with them. If I were you, I'd stay as far away from them as possible."

"Gosh! You guys make it sound like they're criminals or something."

Matt and Andrew looked at each other strangely. I didn't even bother to ask.

"Let's get out of here. If anyone asks, we were helping Mr. Haber clean up the lunch room."

We only had a few more periods to go before the weekend. I was so distracted I couldn't think straight. That story about Vince and his father got me thinking about my father. I wasn't sure when—or if—I would see him again. Or how I would feel when I did. Having a father is important, everybody always says that. And I really needed mine. Maybe I could look at Uncle Carl as my father.

CHAPTER EIGHT
NEW LOOK

I had only seen Uncle Carl's knife collection once before. It was something to lay eyes on as they were of all shapes and sizes. He even had knives that were over one hundred years old. Some were huge and had fancy curved handles for extra grip. Others were small enough to fit in the palm of your hand. It was definitely one of the coolest things I had ever seen. So when Uncle Carl invited me to help polish his knife collection, I took the opportunity.

"Stand back for a second so I can unlock the door," he instructed. "The only other person who knows the combination to this lock is your aunt. And she would kill me if she found out that you or your cousins knew what it was."

I stood back just a few steps and off to the side and placed my hand over my eyes. But my curiosity got the best of me. I split my fingers so I could peek and see what the code was. I got all of the numbers but the last one.

"Hey! Were you peeking?" Uncle Carl exclaimed, turning around.

"Nope! No sir! I didn't see a thing."

"Okay," he replied suspiciously. "Come on in then." He opened the door and light fell on an array of blades.

"WOW! I knew you had a lot of knives, but I didn't know it was this many. They cover the entire wall." My eyes were beaming.

Uncle Carl chuckled. "I've collected a lot more since the last time you were in here. Pretty soon I'm going to have to start hanging them on another wall."

"Can I take this one off over here?" I asked, reaching toward one of the more eye catching ones.

It was about three inches long. The handle was metal with an engraved design of a lion's head on both sides and a button to push for the blade to pop out.

"Sure, but be very careful," Uncle Carl said, watching me closely. "All of these knives are very sharp. If they are not handled carefully they can cause a lot of harm. Especially the one you're reaching for. That's from a knife show that was held in California last year. It's one of only ten ever made. A retired cop made them that small for women to carry in their purses for protection. Production never got off the ground so they just auctioned the ten prototypes."

SNAP! The blade sprung out of the handle with violent force as I pushed the button.

"Michael, be careful!" Uncle Carl shouted.

"WOW! Sorry, You're right, this thing could definitely do some harm."

"Let's put this back on the wall for now," he said, carefully taking the knife out of my hands.

As he placed the weapon back, he looked at me seriously. "I'm glad we have a moment to chat. I wanted to talk about your first few weeks of school. How have things been going?"

I shrugged. "Good I guess. I'm still adapting to the change and trying to make new friends. And then there's the whole bullying thing."

Uncle Carl's eyes widened. "Bullying? Are some of the other kids pushing you around?"

I shrugged again, hoping that he wouldn't make a big deal of it. *Why did I have to bring up bullying?* "Kind of. They just make fun of my clothes and the way I talk. They also call me pizza face because of my acne. Sometimes I just laugh it off. Other times I just act like I didn't hear what they said. It's no big deal." *It's no big deal*, I repeated in my mind, trying to convince myself.

"What about friends? Have you made any?"

"Not really. Well there's Andrew and Matt. They're cool, but they aren't really the most popular guys in school. So hanging out with them isn't very exciting. I'm used to everyone knowing my name and wanting to be around me. It's just not that way here."

Not yet anyway!

Uncle Carl leaned against the doorframe, buffing one of his knives. "Middle school is not a popularity contest, Michael. Perhaps you should focus more on your schoolwork and let your friendships form naturally over time."

No way, I thought. That was terrible advice. "But you get more respect when everyone knows your name, and more girls too. I'd do just about anything to be popular."

He gave me a stern look. "Our words create our world. I'd think twice before saying something like that."

"What do you mean by that?"

"Sometimes, if we say things enough it may actually happen. I don't want you doing *anything* to become popular. Your aunt and I just want you to be true to yourself and always do what's right. I'm sure that's what your mom would have wanted too. You're a good kid and you have a lot going for yourself. Don't worry too much about being popular right now. You have plenty of time for that. Just focus on your schoolwork and making your mom proud by being the young man she raised you to be."

I nodded, mostly just to get him to stop trying to give me a lesson. But maybe he had a fair point. "I hear you, unc."

Uncle Carl was very knowledgeable. Even though I knew he was right, I still felt like I had to do something to make a name for myself.

A shout came from the side door entrance. "Hello! Anyone home?"

"Down here, sweetie!"

Cole and Jake came barreling down the basement stairs, Aunt Sandy slowly behind them.

"Hey pop! What's up Mike?" Cole said.

"Hey, boys. How was karate class?"

"It was cool. We spent the entire class working on our technique for an upcoming tournament. Sensei really wants our division to win this year," Jake replied.

"Do you guys actually fight in these tournaments?" I asked.

"Of course we do!" Jake said.

"Last year one kid broke his nose from getting kicked in the face."

I pondered for a moment. "You guys are going to have to teach me how to fight."

"Karate isn't just about fighting," Uncle Carl said.

"Yeah," replied Cole. "It's also about self-defense, discipline, work ethic, focus, and much more."

"Oh! Well I guess I could learn that stuff too," I said, shrugging. Aunt Sandy and Uncle Carl laughed.

"Well enough about all this fighting and stuff," Aunt Sandy said. "I have some great news, Michael. Your father finally sent some money for me to take you and your sister shopping. Think you're up for that today?"

"Up for it? Of course I am, let's go now!"

I'm sure Aunt Sandy already knew how I would respond. She knew this would cheer me up.

"All right!" she said, matching my excitement. But first, Cole and Jake hit the showers. We'll all have lunch first and then head to the mall."

"How much did he send?" I asked after Cole and Jake left the room.

"Five hundred for you and five hundred for your sister."

I suddenly felt warm inside and my excitement went through the roof.

"Yeah!" I said, throwing my fist in the air. "I should be able to get a lot with that."

"Now I don't know when your father will be able to send this much money again. So we have to be wise with how we spend it, okay?"

"Okay!"

This was the most exciting moment I'd had since we'd been in New York. With some new clothes, people would start noticing me more for sure, and I could finally hang out with the cool kids.

Cole and Jake ran upstairs, showered, and got ready in record time. Even though they already got all their new stuff weeks ago, they were excited to be going shopping with me.

We scarfed down our food like wild animals and piled our plates into the dishwasher. Nicky decided that she didn't want to join us. That was just fine with me; she'd only slow us down.

"Okay, are we ready to bust a move?" Aunt Sandy said, holding her keys and sunglasses.

"Ready!" Cole, Jake, and I responded together.

We all piled into the car and hit the road. The mall was only about fifteen minutes from the house.

"So what do you guys think I should get?" I excitedly asked Cole and Jake.

"Well, you definitely need some new sneakers and some cool jeans," Jake said.

"Yeah, but you need more shirts and sweaters," Cole said. "You can rotate your jeans and sneakers, but you also need a lot of tops. You don't want to be seen in the same clothes only a few days apart." He looked at me seriously. "Didn't you go shopping in Trinidad?" He asked, as if I had never worn new clothes before.

"We wore uniforms in Trinidad," I answered. "We only wore our own clothes to school for trips or special events."

The car slowed down.

"We're here! I've been up since the crack of dawn and I can feel myself getting tired already. So let's see if we can get this done in under two hours, okay?" Aunt Sandy said. She pulled into a parking space and unlocked the doors.

"That's more than enough time, Mom," Jake s

"I hope so!" I replied.

"It is. We know all the best stores. We'll sort you out, Mike. Don't worry about a thing."

"So where shall we go first?" I asked eagerly as we entered the mall, Cole and Jake by my side, Aunt Sandy following behind us.

The mall was three stories high. I thought the malls back in Trinidad were big, but this was definitely the biggest I'd ever seen.

"Come on! Let's check out the sneaker stores first. It's the most important part of your outfit. Everything else is put together around your kicks."

Walking into the first sneaker store was overwhelming. There had to be a couple of hundred pairs of sneakers. I needed a few seconds to get my bearings.

"That pair over there looks cool!" I said, walking towards some orange and black Nikes. As I got closer I realized that I had seen them before. They were the same ones Vince had on the first day of school.

"Yeah, those are fly!" Jake said. "They are one of the hottest releases this year."

"I have to have them."

"They're $120!" Aunt Sandy said, leaning over my shoulder.

I didn't even know she was standing there.

"That's not exactly a wise purchase, Michael."

"I know, but they are so cool. How about this? How about I get one expensive pair and a regular pair? Then I can just focus on getting some clothes to go with them. Deal?"

"You're bargaining with me now?" Aunt Sandy retorted.

"Yup!"

She paused, giving me an awkward stare.

"You kids just don't understand the value of money."

I stared at her with no response. And then she caved. Perhaps it was the helpless look on my face.

"Okay. But this is the most expensive thing you're getting. And we may have to look for some clothes on sale."

I wasn't thrilled about shopping for anything on sale. I wanted all of my new stuff to be the most current, but I absolutely had to have those sneakers.

"Okay, deal!" I said, eagerly walking with the display shoe over to the salesperson, telling him my shoe size. It took everything in me to contain my excitement as he exited the stock room with a box in his hands a few moments later. This was definitely the most expensive thing I was about to own.

New sneakers have a particular smell. As the salesman opened the box, the smell entered my nose like fresh laundry out of the dryer.

"Those are super fresh, Mike," said Cole. "Makes me want a—"

"Don't even think about it!" Aunt Sandy interrupted.

"Shoot! It was worth a shot," Cole said, chuckling.

"These are perfect, sir," I said, wiggling my toes. "I'll take them."

"You got it, young man. You're going to get a lot of attention with these."

"That's exactly what I'm hoping, sir!"

"You be careful, son." He settled my bill and handed me the shoes as Aunt Sandy paid. "Here you go. Have a great day."

"Thank you."

I felt like a million bucks walking out of that store. *To think, I now have the same sneakers as the most popular kid in school.* I grinned until my cheeks were sore.

"I can't wait until Monday," I said to Cole.

"Let's get you some outfits now."

I had two pairs of sneakers, three pairs of jeans, a bunch of tops and I even found a cool book bag to match my new image. All I needed was a haircut.

***

"So I heard you got some pretty cool stuff at the mall?"

"Yup! Wanna see?"

"Sure!"

I knew Nicky didn't care – she was more interested in hair and makeup. That's all she really cared about. But she knew that I would be excited about showing it to her.

She watched patiently as I showed off my new sneakers, shirts, and pants. "Just remember to be yourself," she said. "Don't start acting all conceited just because you have new clothes."

"I won't."

She waved me off. "Well I'm going to bed. You should too. Remember you guys are taking the bus in the morning."

"Goodnight, sis."

With my new outfit draped over the chair, I took one last look in the mirror. No new zits and my haircut was looking great. I was definitely ready for school tomorrow. Things would change for the better, I was sure.

***

"Rise and shine! You boys have to be on the bus in thirty minutes if you're going to make it to school on time."

I wearily looked at the clock and saw that it was another thirty minutes before my alarm went off. Since we were taking the bus starting this week, we had to leave earlier.

I spotted my new outfit and instantly I was wide-awake. I zipped through my morning ritual faster than usual, brushing my teeth and running a hand through my hair, so I could hurry up and get dressed.

I pulled on my jeans, a crisp new shirt, and slipped on my shoes. "These sneakers feel like pillows on my feet," I said, carefully tying my laces.

"Who are you talking to?"

"Oh hey, Cole. I didn't hear you coming up the stairs."

He scoffed. "Probably because you were talking to yourself."

"Just admiring my new kicks, that's all. How do I look?"

"Pretty fresh cuz," he said, eyeing me up and down. "Almost as good as me."

I rolled my eyes. "Whatever! Let's get out of here. I can't wait for school."

Downstairs, Aunt Sandy turned away from the front window holding her favorite mug filled with coffee. "It took you guys long enough. Here are your lunches and some money." She handed us the brown paper bags off the counter and gave each of us $10. "Remember the rules, and please be careful on the bus. Michael, the school has my number at work in case you need to reach me. Bye, boys!" Aunt Sandy hugged us and with coffee and keys in hand, she was gone.

"How far is the bus stop?" I asked, walking out the front gate.

"Its right around the corner," replied Cole.

"Did Mom give you your metro card?" Jake asked me.

"Yup."

"How long is the ride? And how many buses do we have to take?"

"It's about an hour between both buses. Are you nervous or something? What's with all the questions?" Cole asked.

"I'm not nervous," I lied, rubbing my hands together anxiously and straightening my shirt. "Just curious."

Cole seemed to sense that it was more nerves than curiosity. The look on my face coupled with my uncontrollable fidgeting, trying to make sure that my outfit was perfect, must have given it away.

"I'm pretty sure some of our friends will be on the bus too. You can just sit with us," Cole said reassuringly.

"Here it comes." Jake pointed down the block.

As the bus got closer, I could see that this might not be a pleasant ride. It was packed, with standing room only. I was worried about someone stepping on my new sneakers. I felt myself tense up as I hopped off the sidewalk and onto the bus. Getting a ride to school with Aunt Sandy didn't seem like a bad idea right now.

"What's up, guys?" Cole and Jake said, high fiving their friends. "This is our cousin Michael. He just moved here so he'll be riding with us this year."

"Nice kicks!" Someone shouted from the back.

"Thanks." I walked slowly toward the group.

Just a few weeks ago I'd cringe at being introduced to strangers. It always felt like they were connecting the acne spots on my face, or wondering why I wore old clothes. Not today. I could see Cole and Jake's friends checking me out from top to bottom. Suddenly it didn't matter that there was barely any room for anyone on the bus. I was getting some attention and it felt great!

"Yeah, nice outfit," someone else said.

I grinned. "Thanks!"

"See, I said we'd sort you out," Jake muttered to me. "Just wait until you get to your school."

The thought of school suddenly paralyzed me. *What if I don't get the same reaction at school? What if no one even realizes or cares that I have all of this new stuff?*

"Thanks cuz!" I said, sitting down. I kept my composure. I just needed to think a few things over. *Should I walk differently? How should I speak? Should I say anything about my new stuff or wait for someone else to say something first?* I began to sweat.

The bus pulled up to Cole and Jake's stop.

"Later Mike!" Cole and Jake said, getting off the bus.

I looked at my watch. In ten minutes I'd be at school in all of my new stuff. What would people think? More sweat began to appear on my brow.

I had to stay cool. Moments later the bus pulled up in front of the building and I got off with as much confidence as I could muster up. Adding just a bit more of a cool stride to my walk, I made my way inside.

"Hey Mike!"

"What's up, Drew?"

He looked me up and down. "It took me a second to recognize you with all that new gear on. That must have cost a lot."

"Yeah, it did."

I couldn't tell him that everything except my sneakers were from the clearance rack. That would just ruin everything.

"You look brand new. I wish I could wear stuff like that. My parents both have good jobs and they still won't let me buy what I want."

"I guess I'm lucky then. Come on, let's head to class!"

Walking to homeroom must have taken us around three minutes. But in my mind it felt like an eternity. Seeing how the other kids were looking at me made this morning one of the best ever.

CHAPTER NINE
THE DECISION

"You might want to hurry up, Mike," Andrew said. "You'll be late for gym walking at that pace." Andrew ran past me, Matt a few steps behind.

"I'll be right there." These days I didn't rush to do anything. *Whenever I get there, I get there.*

As I strolled into the locker room, I saw that everyone was already dressed.

"Finally. Hurry up and get changed. We have to get on the court first to pick the best squad."

I shrugged. "Go ahead without me, guys."

"But you'll be late," Matt said, turning to look at me dead on. "And you really don't seem to care."

I responded with an indifferent expression. "I don't really!"

Matt and Andrew looked at me like I was a total stranger.

"Whatever, dude," Andrew said, walking out of the locker room, his brow furrowed. Matt walked toward the bathroom. The other students in the aisle of lockers finished changing and piled out as the bell rang. I was alone. Or so I thought…

A loud scream and what sounded like someone kicking in a locker startled me from a few aisles over.

"We have to find those guys. And when we do they are going to pay for what they did to my brother."

I know that voice—the one with a terrifying tone. It was definitely Vince. The hairs on my arms stood up on end.

"We can't just go after Joe and his crew without a plan. And we need at least one other person to roll with us."

That was Tye.

"I don't care! They almost killed Darrel. I can't let them get away with this."

I stopped getting dressed so I could focus and listen closer. My heart began to race. I didn't know who Joe was but whatever he and his crew did to Vince's brother must have been serious.

"We have to find some more people to roll with us. Then we can settle the score," Roy said. He was the third person in the group.

Many different thoughts began rushing through my head. *Is this a chance for me to finally make a name for myself at this school? Being seen with them would definitely help me do that. Maybe I should join them... Is that really me though? What if things get really ugly? What if someone gets hurt? What happened to Matt? What if something like that happens to me?*

I silenced my thoughts, stood up, and walked over to their aisle. This was my perfect opportunity to gain some popularity at this school.

I nodded my head. "You guys looking for some help?"

Vince turned and looked at me in dismay. "How long have you been there? What did you hear?" He walked towards me with clenched fists.

"Relax!" I said, with open palms. This wasn't going the way I thought it would. "I won't say anything. I'm just letting you know that if you guys need some help, I'm in."

"If there's anyone still here you need to get out now!" Mr. Clark yelled from the gym entrance.

Vince leaned in close. His breath was hot and moist. "Fine, you can roll with us, but you better not say anything to anyone. And once you're in, you're in. There's no going back."

Tye stared at Vince. "What? You're letting this foreigner into our squad? He doesn't even know how we roll. He'll just hold us back. And how do we know he won't tell someone?"

"I won't," I said quickly. "You can trust me!" I hoped this was enough for him to back off.

Vince looked at Tye. "But we need bodies. At least he's willing to help us. We can school him in whatever he needs to know."

"I can still hear voices. Out now!" Mr. Clark sounded impatient. He was standing at the end of the aisle.

We broke up and I went back to my locker to finish getting dressed. I exited the locker room alongside Vince and his friends.

"What the heck took you so long? And why did you come out with Vince and his goons?" Andrew asked when I reached him and Matt.

"Nothing! Don't worry about it." I looked away only to see Matt staring at me with a bewildered expression.

"Are you sure? You seem anxious."

"Stop with the third degree!" I said, glaring at them. "I'm good. Let's just play some ball."

Before we could finish one game, the period was over. I must have been really late.

"Hey Mike, wait up!" Andrew hollered as I hurried out of the gym. I was trying to get to our next class as fast as possible so I could just put my head down. I wanted to avoid Andrew's questions. He didn't take the hint.

"Are you sure that you don't want to tell me what's going on?"

"It's nothing bro! Trust me." I was getting frustrated.

"Okay! Whatever you say," he snipped.

We finally made it to class. Somehow Matt had made it there before us. He couldn't take his eyes off of me. It was as if he knew something.

Knock, knock.

Miss Smith again. Great! The last person I wanted to see right now.

We had met every Tuesday and Thursday since I'd been coming here and she still hadn't gotten much out of me. I wished the sessions would just stop. Today was Thursday, so at least I wouldn't see her for another five days.

"Michael!" Mr. Jones said.

"Yeah, yeah! I know the drill," I muttered, gathering my stuff. Miss Smith stood at the door with her fingers clasped together waiting patiently.

"Good morning," she greeted in a bubbly tone as I exited the room.

"Good morning."

Down one flight of stairs and we were at her office.

"Have a seat. So how are things going? Is this another one of your new outfits?

Miss Smith didn't miss much, and she knew how to get you talking.

"Yes it is actually. Things are a little better than before."

She smiled encouragingly. "Just a little?"

"Yeah."

"How so?"

"I feel better about school now. And I'm starting to make some new friends."

"What has you feeling better about school now? And who are these new friends?"

I instantly grew nervous. She knew who Vince and his crew were. And I was sure she knew Vince's story. She couldn't know that I was about to start hanging with them. Even though I couldn't wait for the entire school to find out. Maybe I could get away with just answering the first question and she would move on.

"The other kids don't tease me as much. I actually get compliments about my clothes and sneakers now. I feel a little more confident and relaxed."

"That's great. I'm happy that you're feeling more at ease. And these new friends? Tell me about them."

Shoot! I thought she would just move on.

"I don't think you know any of them."

"Try me."

"Can we talk about something else?"

She looked surprised. "Did I say something?"

"No. I'd just like to talk about something else for now."

"Okay." Miss Smith was caught off guard and agreed to change the subject.

"How are you doing in your classes?"

"I'm pretty sure I'm passing everything."

"Very good. If you keep that up we will need to start looking into some advanced courses. Those always look good on college applications."

"College? Isn't it way too early to start thinking about that?"

She smiled. "It's never too early to start talking about college."

"I guess."

"What about things at home? How are you adjusting?"

Talking about living with Aunt Sandy and Uncle Carl still wasn't easy. I just wasn't completely comfortable with that being my new home yet.

"Any chance we can change the subject again?"

"How about we try to talk this one out?" she pressed.

I paused and took a deep breath.

"I'm adjusting well I guess," I responded reluctantly.

"Why the hesitation?"

"I just don't like talking about anything that makes it seem like I'm comfortable here. Because I'm not!"

She blinked. "But you just said that you're feeling much better about school and that you're making friends."

"Yes, but I still get angry and even sometimes feel depressed when I think about the fact that I live here now." I folded my arms in discontent. "I'd still rather be back home with my friends and family."

"And that is exactly why we need to talk, Michael."

"What do you mean?"

"This is your new home, whether you like it right now or not. It's something that you're going to have to get used to. That's the only way you will be at peace with this change and not feel angry thinking about it."

I huffed. "But what if I never get used to it? What if I'm never happy here or feel comfortable with my new home?"

She looked at me plaintively. "You have to try! It may be hard at times but you have to try."

"How?"

"You might have to get involved in a sport here, or some other extracurricular activity. That will help take your mind off things and it will help you feel connected to something. Continuing to make new friends will also be good for you. I'm glad you said that you're starting to do that, even though you won't tell me who they are." She looked at me suspiciously.

"How is playing sports and making new friends supposed to help me get over that fact that I don't have a mother anymore?" I jabbed.

Miss Smith paused. It's as if a light bulb went off in her head.

"Michael, nothing is going to cause you to get over the loss of your mother. You can only strive to get better with dealing with the fact that she can't physically be here with you anymore. But you will always have the memory of your mom in your heart. And in that way she will always be with you. She's your angel now. As difficult as it may be to heal, you have to give it your best shot. You have a lot of life to live and there are lots of things that you will do to make her proud."

Something about her response stiffened me. I had nothing to say. Would Mom be proud of what I was about to do with Vince and the others? I was beginning to sweat and could feel a trembling feeling brewing, which was certain to be met by tears. Miss Smith saw it too.

"Let's end it here for now. Thank you for opening up a little more today. We are really making some progress. I look forward to seeing you next Tuesday. Have a great weekend, okay?"

"Thank you. I'll try."

I managed to hold back my tears. I still had the rest of the day to get through so I had to keep it together.

As I stepped out into the hallway Vince, Tye, and Roy were walking toward the office.

"You guys got down here fast!" I said as they walked toward me.

Vince had a nervous look on his face. "Did Miss Smith say anything to you? Did she ask you anything?"

"No! Why are you guys being so paranoid?"

"We're just trying to make sure that no one knows what's about to go down." Vince motioned everyone to the other end of the hallway. There was a vestibule down there that no one could see us in unless they were leaving the building.

"Here's how it's going down," he said as we crowded together. "Tomorrow at lunchtime we're going to leave and go to one of Joe's hangouts. We're going to catch him off guard and pay those guys back for what they did to my brother."

"Wait. Why are we going during lunch? Why can't we wait until after school? How do you even know he will be at this place?" I asked, confused.

Tye punched Vince in the shoulder. "I told you he'd have second thoughts," he hissed, glaring at me.

"I'm not having second thoughts!" I backpedaled. "I was just wondering why we had to leave during school hours. I've never cut school before."

"Just do as we say," Vince said, giving me a stern look. "I thought you were cool, man."

"I am, I am!" I said a little too eagerly. "I'm down. So how do you know where to go?"

"I know he'll be there. Every Friday around lunchtime Joe and his crew go to the pool hall up the street." He looked at all of us. "Oh and you guys should bring a weapon."

"Weapon?" I asked. "What kind of weapon?"

This was starting to get really serious and we hadn't even done anything yet.

"See! This is what I was talking about in gym," Tye pressed. "He's not ready."

"I am ready! I just…never mind! Tomorrow. Lunchtime. Bring a weapon. Is that it?"

I couldn't show my concern, but Tye was right, I was having second thoughts.

"Yeah, that's it. You guys bring anything that you can get your hands on. You know I'm always strapped," Vince said, casually lifting his shirt to reveal the butt of a gun.

"*Holy sh—*"

"Lower your voice!" Vince hissed, cutting me off.

All this time I never knew he walked around here with a gun on him. *Who the heck is this guy?*

"Wow, wow, wow. How bad do you want to hurt this dude?" I asked, taking a few steps back.

Vince grabbed my shirt and yanked me towards him. "As bad as it takes! Now are you with us or what?"

"Yeah, Mike," Tye said. "Are you sure you're okay with all of this? We don't need any punks in our group."

If there was a time for me to exit this entire plan, now would be it. How did I get myself into this? Looking around at their hardened faces, I knew I was in too deep. If I backed out now, I might be their next target.

"Sure, guys, I'm in," I heard myself say. I gulped. *How bad can this really be? Vince and his crew may not even be there tomorrow.* Again, I silenced my thoughts. "I'm down for whatever."

"Okay. So it's settled. Tomorrow we'll leave at lunchtime to go and find that fool."

Where the heck am I going to find a concealable weapon?

And then a thought came to me.

Uncle Carl's knives!

"Cool. I'll be ready," I said, more confidently than before.

"What are you boys doing in here?"

"Miss Smith!" I said, startled.

Of course she would show up as we were about to leave.

"Well? Does anyone have an explanation?"

"We were just leaving for class," Vince said.

"Well hurry up. The late bell already rang five minutes ago."

"Yes ma'am!" Vince said, walking away with his head down. Roy followed, then Tye, then me.

"Michael!" Miss Smith said, softly pulling on my shirtsleeve.

"Yes ma'am."

"These aren't those new friends you mentioned earlier, are they?"

"Kind of." My voice was low.

"What do you mean kind of? Either they are or they aren't."

"We were just talking. It's nothing."

"You're sure?" She stepped in front of me, blocking my path from following them. I looked to the side only to see Vince giving me a stern look from a few steps up the hall.

"You know, those aren't the best kids to be hanging around," she said.

"No, those aren't my new friends," I said quietly, my voice low enough that the others wouldn't be able to hear.

She stared at me momentarily, but didn't look convinced. "Okay. Hurry up and get to class then."

I could feel Miss Smith's eyes piercing right through me as I walked away. Turning back to look at her once more, I saw she was standing there with her arms folded tapping her feet. It was clear she was trying to figure out what was really going on. I couldn't worry about that right now, though. One more class and we were out of here. I needed this day to be over so I could get to the house. I'd only have a slim window to get that knife.

I rushed all the way up to the second floor only to see that we had a substitute teacher for our last period.

"What's up, guys?" I greeted Andrew and Matt.

"You're talking to us now? Drew said sharply.

"What do you mean? I never stopped talking to you guys."

"You've been acting funny all day. Ever since you got that new gear, actually. You walk around here like you don't care much about anything anymore."

"I don't know why you're making such a big deal out of this. I still hang out with you guys. We still sit at the same table during lunch. What more do you want from me?"

"Don't do us any favors," Matt said with a dismissive look. My temper flared.

"So you feel the same way?" I asked Matt.

"I'll hold my opinion for now."

"Whatever! Let's just not talk for the rest of the day then."

I didn't want to look at them. I just rested my head until the final bell rang.

I was the first one out of the room. I had to get to the house first.

"Mike. Mike, wait up!" someone shouted from behind me. It was Matt. I was already out of the building making my way to the bus stop.

"What's up? I've gotta hurry up and get home," I said, looking back.

"Hold up. It'll just take a second," Matt said, jogging a little faster.

I waited impatiently.

"I know what you're doing," he said as he got closer to me.

"What are you talking about?" I asked.

"I was in the locker room. I heard everything."

I didn't believe him. "Define everything!"

"I know that you're rolling with Vince and the others to get revenge on Joe and his crew. I was still in the bathroom when you guys were talking. You better be careful. You don't really know what you're getting yourself into."

Rolling my eyes, I said, "Oh please! How bad can it be? Plus, Joe may not even be there. And if he is, so what? We get into a little scuffle and move on. Big deal."

"Scuffle? You have no idea what Joe is capable of. And trust me, there is a reason Joe goes to the pool hall every Friday at lunchtime. He'll be there, along with his clique."

"What's the reason?"

"Let's just say he works for the owner."

"What do you mean? Joe runs the pool hall or something?"

"No, Mike." He pulled me closer and spoke in a low voice. "Joe sells drugs for the owner of the pool hall. He's the biggest drug dealer around here, and he's done some crazy stuff to lots of innocent people."

My stomach was in knots. What did I really get myself into? "You're making this Joe guy sound like some kind of menace to society. Is he really that bad? Or are you just trying to scare me into not going tomorrow?"

"You should be afraid. And I don't think you should be going anywhere with Vince and his crew."

But this is your chance, a little voice inside my head told me. "Well as much as I appreciate the warning, I think I'll be okay. Plus, Vince already said when I'm in with them I'm in. So I don't think I have much of a choice."

"You *do* have a choice, Mike. The same one I made when I left his crew."

"But what if Vince gets upset with me because I want to leave? And Tye. He already thinks I'm soft and that I'm not ready to be down with them."

"Are you?"

"Look, I can't think about this right now. Here comes my bus anyway. I'll see you tomorrow."

"You should listen to me, Mike. You should really think twice about this!" Matt yelled at me as I walked away.

"See you tomorrow, Matt."

I was acting as if I didn't care. But I did. I just didn't know what to do. I felt like I was caught up in something I couldn't get myself out of. I had to shake it off, though. This was my opportunity to make a name for myself. I'd figure out how to disconnect from Vince and his crew another time.

***

Finally home... I had to figure out this weapon situation. I knew exactly where to look but still had a cold feeling of angst inside. Uncle Carl was away on a fishing trip and wouldn't be back until tomorrow morning. As long as no one else was home, I would be able to get my hands on one of the knives from Uncle Carl's collection.

"Hello! Is anyone home?" I said, entering through the side door. I heard nothing.

I walked to the bottom of the living room staircase.

"Is anyone up there?"

Nothing. It was clear.

I made my way down to the basement. It was silent, cool and dark. It felt like someone was ready to pop out from the shadows at any moment. I knew all the numbers to Uncle Carl's lock except one. That couldn't be too hard to figure out.

"Jackpot!" I said on the third try. I was in! I moved quickly to grab one of the smaller knives. One that Uncle Carl wouldn't miss that easily. I grabbed one that fit right in the palm of my hand, and then slid it carefully into my pocket. I just had to lock the door and head upstairs.

Someone sneezed outside.

"Yeah, I'm just glad it was slow enough at the hospital for me to leave. My team has everything under control. I'm going to try to sleep this cold off. I hope your fishing trip is going well." It was Aunt Sandy.

"Shoot! Of all the days she could get sick and have to come home early. Why today?"

She was coming in through the side door, and it sounded like she was talking to Uncle Carl on the phone.

I locked up the room and hurried to make my way upstairs.

"Michael?" Aunt Sandy asked.

She caught me in the basement doorway. *Busted.*

"You're home earlier than usual. Are Cole and Jake home too? And what were you doing in the basement?"

"Uhh yeah! I had a really hectic day at school today so I rushed home to relax. Cole and Jake aren't home yet. I was just using the bathroom down there."

Aunt Sandy eyed me suspiciously and then waved me off.

"Well I'm going upstairs to lie down for a bit. I think I'm coming down with something. There's leftovers in the fridge if you're hungry."

"Okay. I'm going to do my homework while I wait for Cole and Jake to get home."

Aunt Sandy murmured something dismissive as she walked through the living room.

That was too close.

I carefully placed the knife in my book bag and put it in my room. I just had to get through the rest of the day without any questions. Tomorrow was going to be a big day. I had to get my mind ready. *And maybe I shouldn't wear any of my new clothes*, I thought, *just in case things get out of control.*

"Am I really about to do this?" I asked myself.

I began thinking of a few reasons why I shouldn't. Like what Matt said. *Or what if we get caught leaving school? Or worse. What if the cops stop us? Or someone dies? This could go so many different ways.*

I silenced my thoughts again. *Everything will be fine. We might get into a fight, but so what? That's what guys do.* I just needed to get some rest, I decided.

But then a disturbing thought entered my mind.

What would Mom have thought?

CHAPTER TEN
THE MEETING

"Michael! Are you in there? Michael! It's time to get up. Open the door. You're about to get left," Cole said, wiggling the locked door handle.

I slid out of the bed and dragged myself to open the door.

"Hey! What time is it?" I was still half asleep and could barely stand straight.

"It's 5:45. What's going on with you? Usually you're dressed and ready to go by now."

"I don't know. I must have been more tired than I thought last night."

The truth was I couldn't sleep. I had been up all night replaying the different scenarios of today. Was I making the right decision? I couldn't tell Cole.

"Hurry up so we can get out of here. We have about fifteen minutes to catch our bus."

"Okay. I'll be right down."

I rummaged through my drawers to find some of my old clothes, just in case things got out of hand. At least I wouldn't be worried about getting anything messed up. I managed to put something together and headed downstairs to brush my teeth. Cole and Jake were ready to leave five minutes ago.

"What are you still doing here? And what are you wearing?" Nicky asked, coming out of the bathroom.

"What do you mean what am I wearing? Clothes!"

"You know what I mean, smart-aleck. You haven't worn anything like that since you went shopping. You look like you're going to the park or something."

"Just forget about it. I didn't feel like wearing anything fancy today. That's all."

"Michael, come on! Our bus will be pulling up any minute now," Cole yelled from the kitchen.

"Be right down!"

I brushed my teeth, washed my face, and bolted downstairs. Cole, Jake, and I ran down the block hoping we'd catch the same bus we'd taken to school for the last few weeks. We made it just in time.

"I just noticed what you are wearing. You feeling okay?" Cole asked.

"Yeah cuz. You don't seem like yourself today," Jake added.

"I'm fine. Why is everyone stressing over my outfit? I just didn't feel like going all out today, okay? Can I do that?" I asked, sarcastically.

Cole and Jake looked at each other, surprised at my response.

"Chill out, cuz. We were just asking. No need to get all fired up," Jake said.

The day wasn't even in full swing yet and I was already feeling stressed. I couldn't deal with all these questions.

"Whatever!"

I put my headphones on and zoned out. Staring out the window and listening to music was probably the best way to be left alone. Cole and Jake turned around to talk to their friends.

"Mike," someone said, tapping me on the shoulder. It was Cole. I had fallen asleep.

"See you later on. This is our stop."

"Later guys!" I said, yawing.

The closer I got to school, the more nervous I felt. My heart could have popped out of my chest at any moment. Thoughts of whether or not I should go with Vince and the others began filling my head. This feeling was very uncomfortable.

I had to silence these thoughts again; I couldn't let them deter me. Just being seen with Vince and his crew would do wonders for my popularity.

As our bus approached the front of the building I imagined how different things would be when all this was over. I'd be one of the most popular kids at this school. I'd sit at the popular table with Vince and the others. Everyone would look up to me because I'd be in the "in" crowd. Girls would want to date me, guys would want to be me. The thought of everyone knowing my name felt amazing. Today was the first day of a new and better chapter here. I just had to get through the next few hours. That was all that it would take.

"Good morning, Michael!" I heard walking toward the staircase. It was Mrs. Green. She was surrounded by all of the school safety officers. I guess they were having some kind of meeting.

"Morning Mrs. Green."

"Come over here for a second."

Caught off guard, I froze. Why would she say that?

"The late bell is about to ring," I called, my feet planted in place. "Maybe later?"

"It's okay. I'll give you a late pass. Come on over here," she replied, dismissing the officers.

It was strange walking over there with a knife in my bag. It felt like the school agents were looking at me differently. I had to act normal, though. I couldn't ignore the principal.

"Come into my office, we haven't caught up in some time."

God, I hope this isn't like another session with Miss Smith. I can't deal with this right now.

"So how are things going? How are you adjusting here?"

My shoulders slumped as I realized this meeting was exactly what I didn't want: small talk.

"Everything is fine. I'm adjusting okay."

"Are you sure? Is there anything I can help you with?"

"No. Nothing I can think of."

"How about your sessions with Miss Smith? She mentioned something to me about moving you into a more advanced course because of your grades. That's pretty awesome."

"Yeah I guess."

I couldn't think of anything other than lunch period. I hope Mrs. Green wasn't expecting much out of me. This was about all she was going to get.

"Well, we can discuss that another time. You can head up to class."

I think she got the hint.

I got a late pass from the secretary and headed up to homeroom. When I walked in, everyone was reading something on a piece of paper. There was one on my desk too.

"What's this?" I asked Andrew.

"It's a letter from Mrs. Green. Every student in the school has to read and sign it."

"A letter from Mrs. Green? I was just in her office. She didn't mention anything to me."

"What were you doing in Mrs. Green's office?" Andrew asked.

"Yeah Michael. What were you doing in the principal's office?" Tye echoed from the back of the class.

"Nothing!" I said, waving off the both of them.

"Okay guys. That's enough. I need everyone to read the handout and sign it. I will collect them as you leave for your next class," Miss Rose said.

I sat down to read the letter.

Dear student,

It has been brought to our attention that one of our old students was severely beaten up a few blocks away from school and is now in serious condition at a local hospital. Darrel Rogers graduated from...

"Wait a minute! Darrel Rogers?" I said under my breath.
Vince's brother...

I immediately turned around to look at Vince. He had balled up his note and was squeezing it as if he was expecting

118

water to appear. His face was bright red and I could see bulging veins popping out of his neck. He was fuming. I turned back around to finish the letter.

...this school two years ago. One of our neighbors was watering her lawn when she saw two groups of teens begin to argue and then fight. She ran inside to call the police but before they could arrive, the damage had already been done. Darrel was stabbed several times and left for dead. By the time the police and ambulance arrived on the scene, Darrel had already lost a lot of blood. We hope that he fully recovers but this cannot happen again. This all took place during school hours and we have now found out that some of our students were present at the time of the incident.

From the moment you enter this building, we are responsible for you until the last bell of the day rings and you go home. If you leave during the day and something happens to you, we will be held accountable. But even worse than that is the trouble you will be in. Leaving this building under any circumstances is not permitted during school hours. Unless your class is going on a trip accompanied by a member of staff, you are to remain inside until dismissed at the end of the day. Anyone caught breaking this rule will be subject to a superintendent suspension.

Please sign the bottom of this form in agreement to these terms.

There was an awkward silence in the room. Everyone knew who Darrel was, and we all knew that Vince was his little brother. The bell rang and everyone left for our next class. I was in a daze. The timing of this letter couldn't have been worse.

Vince pulled Tye, Roy, and myself to one side.

"We're still good right?" he said in a cautious tone as we entered the stairwell.

"We're good," Tye replied. Roy echoed the same thing.

"So we are just going to ignore this letter," I said with slight sarcasm.

"Screw that letter. We're going, and you are too. Or are you too much of a punk?" Vince said.

I gulped and shook my head.

"On our way down to the lunchroom we will sneak out of the side entrance by the gym."

"The gym! That exit is near Miss Smith's room. Can we go out another way?" I asked.

"No! That's the best exit for us to take if we don't want to be seen," Tye replied.

"So it's settled," Vince said.

The next couple of periods ticked by, minute by minute. I couldn't keep my eyes off the clock. I felt as if every minute that passed was a minute closer to my impending doom. Scenes of what could happen flashed before my eyes. I envisioned myself being dragged off to juvenile hall, or put in foster care because Aunt Sandy and Uncle Carl were determined as unfit guardians. Twice I considered backing out, but I convinced myself to stick to the plan.

The last minute eventually arrived and the bell rang. Vince gave us a signal and we gathered at the back of the class to head downstairs.

"Have you got your weapons?" He said to us softly.

Tye, Roy, and myself nodded in agreement and were ready to start moving

***

"Hey Mike, wait up. Why are you walking so fast?" Andrew said, tugging at my book bag.

"And where are you going with them?" Matt said, slowing me down from Vince and the others.

"Let go of my bag," I said, wrenching it away from them. They looked confused. "I've got to take care of some stuff. I'll be back before the period is over."

"Back? Where are you going?" Andrew asked, confused. "We're not allowed to leave the building, remember?"

"Never mind that! I'll be right back."

We were already downstairs in the hallway by the gym leading out of the building, but Andrew and Matt continued to follow us.

"Mike, let's go!" Vince hollered from the other end of the hall.

"So you're hanging out with them now?" Andrew said, upset.

"I'm just going to the pool hall. Why don't you join us?"

"To the pool hall? Are you crazy?" Matt said.

"Relax! It's not that serious," I said, shrugging off Matt's statement.

"Come on, Drew. Let's go!" I said.

"Heck no! Did you read the letter from Mrs. Green this morning? What if we get caught?"

"We won't get caught. Stop being a punk."

"I'm not a punk. And I'm definitely not going with you guys. You shouldn't go either Mike, and you know it."

"Mike, we gotta go!" Vince was getting increasingly frustrated.

I paused and thought about it for a few seconds. Mrs. Green did say that we shouldn't leave the building. But I was finally hanging out with the cool kids. My mind was made up, I couldn't say no.

"I'm going. How bad can it be?"

I turned and began walking towards the exit door.

Matt grabbed my book bag and I turned around again, angry.

"You've changed a lot since you bought those new clothes!" he exclaimed. "You're acting like a jerk now, just like the rest of your new crew."

I yanked my bag out of his hands again. "What are you talking about? This is not my new crew. I'm just going to the pool hall with them. We're still friends."

"I don't really know if we are, Mike. If we were friends, you wouldn't call Drew a punk and you would listen to my advice. I'm trying to help you so you don't get into trouble, or worse."

"Oh whatever! Stop making a big deal out of this. I'm going. I'll catch up with you guys later."

I turned away from Matt's hardened face and ran down the hall to meet up with the others.

***

When we arrived at the pool hall, there were only about five people there. There was hardly any light and it reeked of beer. The furniture was seriously dated and there was only one pool table. This was more like a pool room, not a pool hall.

"I'm here to see Joe," Vince announced to the guy behind the bar.

"He's not here."

Vince backed away from the bar and rejoined our group.

"Tye," Vince hissed, eyeing two guys at the far end of the room.

"Yeah?" Tye replied.

"See those two dudes over there?"

"Yeah. Why?"

"They haven't stopped staring at us since we walked in."

We looked to the other end of the room to see who he was talking about. And just like that, the two guys stood up and left through a side door, leaving at least half a plate of food behind.

"Who were those guys?" I asked.

"I have no idea, but if I had to guess, I'd say they were with Joe," Vince said.

"What are we gonna do?" I whispered.

"Let's just wait for Joe to show up," Vince said. "He'll be here eventually."

Almost thirty minutes later the period was almost over and still, no sign of Joe. We needed to leave soon if we didn't want anyone to know we left. Our plan was to walk in the back door when everyone was changing classes so we could just fall in line.

"Shoot!" Vince said, looking at the time.

"Of course he wouldn't be here on the day we show up. Looks like we'll have to wait until Monday, guys."

As we were walking down the block, we saw those two guys from the pool hall again. They were standing on the corner acting as if they were waiting for someone. Were they waiting for us? As we got closer they looked into a nearby store and began signaling a group of people to come outside.

"I have a funny feeling about this," Roy said in an uneasy tone.

"What do you mean? I don't know them. Do any of you know who they are?" Tye said.

"No," we all replied.

"It looks like something is about to go down," Roy said.

We continued walking towards them. More guys exited the store as we drew closer. Whatever was about to go down was going to be major.

Suddenly twenty people surrounded us. Something was definitely going down. We just didn't know it would involve us.

"Guys! Is that Joe?" Tye said.

"Crap! It sure is," Vince said, in a defeated voice.

I don't think this is how he imagined confronting Joe.

All this time we had been waiting for Joe, and just like that, he was standing right in front of us.

"I heard you losers were looking me," Joe said in a cocky voice.

I looked over at Vince. His face got red and he started to shake. He was definitely about to explode. His fists clenched, loosened, clenched again, and then loosened.

"How the heck did you know we were looking for you?" Tye asked.

"Come on man! You know I have eyes and ears all over this town. I know everything that's about to go down around here way before it actually does."

"So what? You were hiding?" Tye challenged.

Joe's crew started gearing up for a fight. One guy began shadow boxing and flexing his muscles. I had my eye on him and a few of the others, but I couldn't see everyone else. This could all go down any second. My heart hammered in my chest. I should have listened to Matt and Andrew and stayed in the building. But I couldn't think about that right now. All I could think about was who to hit first if we started rumbling.

"Now you know I don't have to hide from any of you chumps. I'm just strategic, that's all. You of all people should know that." Joe directed his attention to Vince. "Your brother thought he could drop out of my squad and get away from me without paying the consequences. But I got him eventually, and he got dealt w—"

Vince immediately lunged at him and punched him in the face. Joe fell back, holding his jaw, stunned and furious.

Then it all kicked off. I hit the guy closest to me; fists were flying everywhere. I tried to reach into my bag for my knife. But I don't think that ever happened.

The next moment I awoke in a daze on the floor inside a building. I had no idea where I was. Above me a sign read, *Al the Butcher's Best Cuts.* A man was sitting over me in a white apron. He was patting blood off my face.

"What happened?" I asked the butcher. I didn't remember much after the mirage of fists.

"You guys got beat up pretty badly. It had to be at least four or five of them against each one of you. I managed to pull you in from the crowd and I locked the door so they couldn't get in, but I couldn't help the other guys."

"Did you notice one of my friends that had on a red cap?" I asked. My tongue felt large and swollen in my mouth.

"Yes."

"That's Vince. What happened to him? Did you see? Where is he? Where is the crew?"

"Whoa, whoa, whoa. Slow down, kid! You're lucky you got outta there alive. I called the cops after I dragged you in here. As soon as those thugs heard the sirens, they all ran off like a bunch of roaches."

I jumped up and tried to leave the butcher shop but the door was still locked. My head was pounding and I felt a little light-headed. My body was aching from all the kicks and punches. I sat back down to see if my head would stop spinning long enough for me to make it out of there. That's when I noticed all of the blood on my clothes. It's a good thing I didn't wear a new outfit.

"Why does my head hurt so much?" I asked.

"One of them hit you really good. He knocked you out cold. That's how I was able to get you in here. You fell right in front of my door."

I needed to find the crew. I asked the butcher to let me out so I could go look for everyone. I tried to stand, but the butcher held me down.

"You don't look so good kid. I'm a retired boxer. You might need to get checked out to see if you have a concussion."

"I need to go. Can you please unlock the door?"

"Hey kid. I hope you're not going to do anything stupid. You should go back to school or go home. But whatever you do, don't go looking for any more trouble."

"Whatever, mister! I gotta find my friends. Can you just let me out?"

After he unlocked the door to his shop, sirens were blaring outside. They were close. I had to get out of there.

I looked up and down the block but I didn't see anyone. I looked down at the sidewalk and there was blood everywhere. There was no way I could hide what just happened so I definitely was not going back to school. Maybe if I left now I could make it home before anyone else and just get rid of my clothes.

I'll stop by Vince's apartment building before I get on the bus, I thought. I had a feeling that's where everyone might be.

"Yo Mike! Over here," I heard as I was walking toward his building.

It was Vince and the others. They were in the park across the street facing the back of the school.

"Fine place for you guys to meet up considering we are supposed to be *inside* the school. Are you guys okay?" I said, walking toward them.

"Relax, Mike! Mrs. Green's office is on the other side of the building and so are all the safety officers. No one can see us here." Vince replied.

"Oh man! I thought I got it bad. You guys are just as bloody and bruised up as me," I said. Vince's cheek was red and swollen, Tye's forearms were scratched up and bloody, and Roy had a blackened eye.

"Those fools are lucky they caught us off guard. Luckily for them, I didn't have time to reach for my gun. Someone would have definitely been going to the hospital." Vince said.

"So what are you guys going to do now?" I asked.

"We are going to get those clowns back, every single one of them. Especially Joe," Tye said.

"You guys can deal with the rest of them. Joe is mine. He is gonna pay big time," Vince said. "Are you still down with us, Mike?"

I was speechless. I wanted to help but this was definitely not what I expected. But I felt like I couldn't say no. I was this close to be down with the most well known crew at school. Backing out now would be a waste.

"I'm down," I said.

"Cool! We'll get those guys on Monday," Vince said.

We all split up and I headed home. I started to think of how I was going to get rid of my clothes, and what I was going to say about the cuts and bruises all over my face and arms. I could hide everything else, but those injuries were too obvious.

***

The bus came almost as soon as I got there. I got on and started thinking of a plan. I needed to make sure no one saw my clothes, but I also needed to make sure that if anyone saw me at home this early it was for good reason. *I know! I'll say I'm really banged up from playing football during gym and that I just couldn't make it through a full day because of the pain.* That could also be the reason I have all these cuts and bruises, I realized, thinking quickly. *Football is a pretty rough sport. Who wouldn't believe that?*

I got to my stop and got off the bus. I looked down the block to make sure I didn't see anyone's car parked in front of the house. Sometimes that's where Aunt Sandy would park if she came home early, just in case she had to make a quick run somewhere. The coast was clear, for now. I still had to make sure no one saw me walking to the house. Some of the neighbors were real gossipers, just like a bunch of parrots.

I managed to get in the house without being seen. When I looked at my face in the bathroom mirror I saw how bad it really was. I had a few cuts on my forehead and a huge purple spot on my right temple. I guess that's where whoever knocked me out hit me. There was no way I could hide that.

Taking a shower was going to be tough, but I had to get washed up. I grabbed some clothes from my room so I could get dressed as soon as I got out of the shower.

"Ouch! Ouch! Ouch!" I said as the cold water hit my skin. I thought it would be better if it was cold, but I guess it really didn't matter. Anything touching my skin was excruciating.

"Michael is that you?" a voice said from the hallway.

It was Nicky! What the heck was she doing home?

"Michael! I know you're in there. What are you doing home so early? It's not even noon yet. And I know you didn't have a half-day. Come out here right now," Nicky yelled as she stood outside the bathroom door.

I jumped out of the shower, dried off, and got dressed immediately.

"Shh! Why do you have to be so loud?" I said as I opened the bathroom door.

"I'm the one asking the questions," Nicky replied. "And since I'm asking, what happened to your face?

"Someone hit me while we were playing football during gym class."

"You're such a liar. And why are you wearing a long sleeve T-shirt? It's not cold in here."

"Okay. Okay. Gosh! You are so nosy. Just stop yelling. I got jumped today."

"What do you mean? You got jumped in school?" Nicky said in a concerned tone.

"No. I got jumped up the block from school. I was helping a friend and when we were leaving we bumped into this guy that my friend has beef with."

"Who is this friend? The only person I've ever heard you talk to on the phone is Andrew."

"You don't know him. You can't say anything, Nicky. I can't go back to school looking like this. Plus my clothes were covered in blood from all these cuts."

"So that's why you were wearing those old clothes today? Boy are you in for it."

"What? I just told you. You can't say anything."

"What am I supposed to say, Michael? You just told me you cut school and that you got into a fight with some kids you probably shouldn't have been hanging out with in the first place."

"Just act as if you don't know anything."

"So you want me to lie for you?"

"Yeah! Just like I would lie for you," I said.

Nicky looked at me in disgust. "Fine. But you better not get into any more drama with those so-called friends of yours. Because I'm not backing you up if anything like this happens again."

I sighed, relieved. "Thanks, Nicky."

I stayed inside for the rest of the day. There was no way I was going to risk going back to school. What if someone found out? Would we be suspended? Expelled? I just couldn't deal with it today.

A few hours later when Jake and Cole got home from school, I prepared myself for the barrage of questions.

"Wow! What the heck happened to you?" Jake asked.

"I was playing football during gym class today."

"Were you playing full contact? That's a massive bruise on your face."

"The guys on the other team were huge and I took a couple of hard tackles," I said as I chuckled. I had to make my story as believable as possible. Jake and Cole were known to come home with cuts and bruises from playing outside too. So this shouldn't have come as a big surprise.

"You look like a train hit you!" Cole said.

"Okay. Okay. Can we just drop it?" I said.

We played video games for a couple of hours, and despite my pounding headache, I was able to relax and get my mind off what had happened earlier that day.

The door slammed upstairs.

"Boys, come on up, it's time for dinner," Aunt Sandy said from the kitchen. "I picked up a pizza!"

It was time to face the music. We walked upstairs and went straight to the dining room. I sat down and placed my head in my right hand. It was a meager attempt at covering the bruise on my head. But that was getting really uncomfortable. By the time the food was on the table, I couldn't hide it anymore.

"Michael! What happened to you?" Aunt Sandy asked.

"What do you mean?"

"Don't play dumb with me. What happened to your face?"

"Oh that. It's nothing. We were playing football today and I took a couple of hits. That's all."

For a few seconds everyone went silent. Nicky looked at me from the corner of her eye.

"Are you sure you are telling me the truth? Do I need to call your school on Monday?"

"No! You don't have to do that." I swallowed. "Everything is fine. It's just from playing football. I promise."

Aunt Sandy gave me the most suspicious look I had ever seen. It pierced right through me. I don't think she believed a word I was saying.

"Okay then. If you say that's all it is, I guess I have no choice but to believe you."

When we had finished eating, I was the first to get up from the table. I put my things in the dish drainer and went downstairs to use the bathroom.

As I was passing back through the kitchen to go upstairs and lay down, Aunt Sandy and Uncle Carl were talking about something that seemed rather important. They stopped as soon as I entered. I didn't really think anything of it so I said goodnight.

"Going to bed so early, Michael?" Aunt Sandy said.

"Yeah. I'm kind of tired from school today. I think I need some rest."

Aunt Sandy gave me a funny look.

"Okay, goodnight, kiddo," said Uncle Carl. He and Aunt Sandy looked at each other as I left the room.

I finally made it to bed but falling asleep wasn't easy. After tossing and turning, I must have only slept for about four solid hours.

When I woke up the next morning my body was extremely sore. *I hope this wears off before the weekend is over.*

Everyone was up and active in the house already. I eagerly followed the smell of bacon and eggs to the kitchen. There was a calm and normal atmosphere in the house on Saturday.

That's when Uncle Carl emerged from the basement with a confused expression.

"Hey Dad. What's wrong?" Cole asked.

"Have you seen one of my switchblades lying around anywhere?"

I felt my face flame.

"Nope," Cole said.

"What about you two?" Uncle Carl said, looking at Jake and me.

"Nope!" we both replied.

"I was polishing them last night and I think one is missing. I checked everywhere and I can't seem to find it."

Shoot! I never put the knife back. I wasn't sure if Uncle Carl really didn't know where the knife was or if he was faking it to give whoever took it a chance to come forward. They did that kind of thing in this family.

"Come on guys. We're going to be late for karate." Aunt Sandy said.

I was the first out the door. As nervous as I was, I had to remain as calm as possible. If Cole or Jake found out I took the knife, they would definitely tell on me.

Luckily, we made it to karate and through the rest of the weekend like nothing ever happened.

CHAPTER ELEVEN
THE INCIDENT

It was 5:00 a.m. on Monday morning and my nerves were flaring. Uncle Carl never brought up the missing knife again so I wasn't too worried about it anymore. Maybe he thought he lost it on his fishing trip or something. I just needed it for one more day. After the score was settled with Joe's crew, I'd put it right back. We all went through our normal morning routine and headed off to school.

"Hey Mike, I need to talk to you for a second," Andrew said as soon as he saw me.

"I know what's going down after school today. I'm warning you. You shouldn't go with those guys. They are getting ready to do something really bad and you don't want to be involved in any of it."

"How do you know what's about to happen today?"

"Matt called me over the weekend and told me he heard Vince strategizing with Tye. Then he said that he saw Vince making sure that everything was in working order with his gun on the rooftop of his building. He said something about making sure it was ready to go if necessary."

"Umm, I wouldn't worry about it too much man," I said, waving Andrew off.

"Why are you being so naïve?"

I sighed, and instantly turned defensive. "I can handle myself, Andrew. Plus do you see what one of those chumps did to my face? I've gotta get them back. Naïve? I don't think so. I'm just standing up for myself and getting my own revenge."

"I don't think you realize how ridiculous you sound."

"I'm perfectly fine, bro."

"No, you're really not! You shouldn't have been there in the first place. This isn't you, this isn't your beef, it's Vince's. Let him handle it. If Tye, Roy, and whoever else he gets to tag along want to help him that's on them, but you don't have to."

"Whatever! If you really understood then you'd realize that I have no choice."

"You're just going because you want to be down with his crew. You're not like them. I don't know what has come over you but I won't try to stop you anymore. If you want to die or end up in jail, it's on you."

"Stop saying that crap. Nothing like that is gonna happen. We're just gonna find those guys, beat them down, and everything will be settled."

"You wish it was that easy," Andrew said.

"We should really get to class. Can we just stop discussing this?" I snapped.

I walked into the homeroom. "Hey fellas!" I said to the crew.

"Hey Mike," everyone replied. A warm sense of acceptance engulfed my body. I felt that I belonged. The cool kids acknowledged me as one of their own. I was one of them now...

"You ready for this afternoon?" Vince asked.

"Yup!"

"What about your weapon?" he asked quietly.

"Got that too," I replied.

"Cool. I know where Joe and his crew will be today. Someone told me that they're always in front of the corner store by his apartment building on 63rd street. We will definitely catch them off guard this time," Vince said.

Mrs. Green walked in the room, leaving three safety agents in the hallway. It's as if they were her bodyguards.

"Good morning class," she said.

"Good morning Mrs. Green," we all responded.

"Would the following students please step out into the hallway? Vince Rogers, Tye Cummings, Michael Bell, and Roy Anderson."

My heart stopped. *They know.* This was all about to be over before it even started.

We all got up, eyeing each other nervously, and went out into the hall. The safety agents and Mrs. Green pointed to the elevator and we all got in. No one said a word. But we all knew what this was about. We exited the elevator and entered Mrs. Green's office.

"Take a seat at the table, please," one of the safety officers instructed, pointing us to a big round table in the center of the room.

Mrs. Green stood before us.

"Last Friday all of you went missing during lunch. From the looks of it, you all have been fighting. I know that you all read the letter I handed out about leaving during school hours. You are all in a lot of trouble as it stands. But I am going to give you a chance to tell me what's going on. I hope that you'll take this opportunity to come clean before anything worse happens. Do any of you want to go first?"

There was a deadly silence.

"If any of you would like to say something, now is the time."

Still nothing. The guilty silence lingered.

Mrs. Green had that look on her face. She was determined to get the information she needed.

"Okay. Since no one wants to tell me anything, I am going to speak with each of you individually until someone says something. Let's go, Tye."

Tye got up and began walking to another room connected to Mrs. Green's office. As he was walking away he looked over at Vince who shook his head from side to side. Vince's expression didn't need an explanation: That was his way of telling him to not say a thing about what was going down after school or about what happened on Friday.

The two of them were in that room for almost twenty minutes. When Tye came out, he was sweating bullets. But Mrs. Green didn't have the info she wanted. At least that's how she was acting.

"This will all end when someone decides to tell me what I want to hear. I've got all day if you want to keep playing this game. But until someone speaks up, you are all going to be sitting here. And if no one says anything I will call your parents to come and pick you up at the end of today, after I have suspended you all indefinitely. You're up, Roy."

Mrs. Green questioned Roy for about the same time, and still, not a word.

It was Vince's turn. Half the day had gone. I couldn't have Mrs. Green call Aunt Sandy. If she found out what was going on, that would be the end of me.

Vince came out of that room looking even angrier.

"You're up, Michael," Mrs. Green said.

As soon as she said that, Vince made a run for the door on the other side of the room. The safety agents weren't manning that door so he was able to slip out. With everyone franticly focusing on getting him back inside, all of the attention was off the rest of us. We panicked. Tye and Roy decided to make a run for it too, darting to one of the front exit doors ahead. I followed right behind them.

I made it to the staircase and that's when it happened. The knife I thought was securely in my pocket fell out. I ran to pick it up but as soon as I bent down to get it, one of the other agents grabbed me by my arm. *Why the heck did I even turn back for the knife? I should have just kept going.* I thought.

"Let's go!" he said.

It was all over—for me, anyway. The others got out and were going to look for Joe. It was about to go down and I was about to miss everything because of one stupid mistake.

"Have a seat, and if you even think of moving, we are going to have a serious problem," the agent said.

"Agent Connolly to Mrs. Green, Agent Connolly to Mrs. Green," he said over the walkie talkie.

"Go ahead, Agent Connolly."

"I have one of them in your office right now, over." He looked at me. "What's your name, kid?"

"Michael," I replied softly.

"Michael what?"

"Michael Bell," I replied with an attitude.

"He says his name is Michael Bell."

"Roger that, Agent Connolly. I'm on my way back to you now. Don't take your eyes off of him. And would someone call 911?"

"Roger that!" Agent Connolly said.

"Aww man! You're calling the cops?" I said out loud.

"You be quiet! You kids think we don't know what's going on around here but we do. Do you even realize how serious this is?" He grabbed my arm hard—probably harder than he intended. This didn't look good, not one bit. "Where did you get this knife?"

There was no point trying to hide it now.

"I took it from my Uncle's collection."

"You can be arrested for having this on you. What were you thinking, kid?"

Mrs. Green walked in seconds later, panting heavily from the running.

"Michael," she said, disappointment etched on her face. That was the worst part. "You need to tell me everything that is about to go down. I need names, I need to know where, and I need to know *why*."

"But Mrs. Green, I don't know anything," I said.

"Michael! Now is not the time to lie to me. Someone could get hurt or even die out there. Tell me what you know right now!" she yelled.

"I'm telling you, I don't know anything."

140

"If you don't know anything then why were you running out with them and why are you carrying this knife?" Her brows furrowed. "You are one of my smarter, well-behaved students. But lately something has come over you. I've been watching you hang out with Vince and his crew. I've seen how you straggle along in the hallway between classes, and how you've been carrying yourself over the last few weeks. You're not the same humble, softly-spoken kid who came to this school at the start of the year. You've somehow become more arrogant, self-centered, and brash, acting like you don't care about anything. I know this has been a tough transition for you, and I want to help you, Michael. But right now, you need to help me first. Tell me what I need to know so we can resolve this situation without anyone getting hurt or worse."

I sighed. Mrs. Green's words cut straight to my heart. *Is that really the person I've become?* This was the most embarrassed I'd felt in a long time. And to think, Mom sent Nicky and me here to get away from this type of foolishness.

I couldn't take it anymore. I talked.

"They are going to find some kid named Joe. We got into a brawl with him and his crew on Friday. Vince had beef with Joe because he beat up his brother about a week ago."

"Keep going. What else do you know? Where are they going?"

"Vince said something about going to a corner store on 63rd street. He said that's where Joe will be today."

Mrs. Green looked at Agent Connolly. "Call the precinct and let them know that some of our kids are heading over to that store on 63rd. Explain the situation to them and let them know to be ready for anything."

"Yes ma'am," Agent Connolly said.

"And tell him that our kids are out there, and to please be extra careful!" Mrs. Green shouted as Agent Connolly went running.

"Michael, I'm calling your aunt."

I couldn't believe how this was unfolding. *I'm sure I'll be grounded for the rest of the year. What was I thinking? All this just to be friends with some guys who don't seem to care about anything.*

"Your aunt is going to be here soon," Mrs. Green said when she hung up the phone. "You are going to sit right there until she arrives."

POP, POP... POP!

"What in the world was that?" Mrs. Green said, running to the window.

The hair on my arms rose. I knew exactly what it was—it was gunfire. Three shots rang out.

Police sirens were blaring everywhere.

This was serious.

"Those sounded like gunshots," I said.

"Michael, you get down," Mrs. Green instructed as she locked the door and turned out the lights. I got down on the floor under her desk. My heart was pounding.

Moments later, there was a banging on the door. Mrs. Green peeked to see who it was. When she opened it, there were two of the other safety agents holding Tye and Roy by their collars.

"It's Vince. He's been shot," one of the agents said.

I couldn't believe what I was hearing.

"We already called an ambulance," the other agent said.

Mrs. Green grabbed Tye and Roy and motioned them to the desk I was under. "Someone tell me what happened."

"We followed them to the end of the block," one of the agents explained. "We were close behind them but we couldn't catch up. As soon as Vince turned the corner on 63rd street and the other guy saw him running in his direction, he pulled out a gun and started shooting at Vince. The guy got two shots off. One caught Vince in the leg. Vince reached for his gun as he was falling to the ground, but before he could get to it, a third shot came out of nowhere. It was a cop. He shot that guy Joe down from the other corner. I think he's dead. One of the other agents stayed back with Vince and the cops. We got these two and brought them back."

"Wow!" I exclaimed.

Mrs. Green turned and glared at me, and I quieted. This wasn't something to be excited about, I realized. Not at all.

I had no idea that this would end so badly. And to think, I almost went with them. That could have been me. It could have been any of us who were shot—or killed. What the heck was I thinking? There no way being cool was this important. *I may have lost two good friends. Matt and Andrew may never speak to me again. I lied to my family, I stole something that didn't belong to me, and now I may get kicked out of school or worse. This is definitely not worth it.*

It was a sobering wake-up call.

An hour later, when the school was lifted from its lockdown, Aunt Sandy rushed in, a nervous wreck.

"Michael. Michael. Where is he? Where's Michael Bell?" she asked one of the agents.

"Right over here!" Mrs. Green said, waving Aunt Sandy down.

"I'm so sorry. I made a huge mistake. I'm so sorry," I said.

"It's okay, Michael. It's okay. Everything is going to be fine." Aunt Sandy pulled me in and hugged me tighter than ever.

"I believe this belongs to you, sir," Agent Connolly said, holding out the knife. "Sir?"

I looked up to see who he was talking to. It was Uncle Carl.

Uncle Carl looked down at the weapon. "Thank you. Yes it does," he said, looking at me disappointed but relieved.

"We're going to have to hand this over to the police as evidence," Agent Connolly added.

Uncle Carl grunted, glaring at me.

"I'm sorry, Uncle Carl. You tried to warn me but I didn't listen. I should have confessed when you asked about the knife over the weekend. And now look at this mess. I'm really sorry."

His face softened. "Come here son! We will work all of this out. Your aunt and I are here for you."

Uncle Carl's response wasn't what I expected. I just knew he was going to let me have it, and really make me feel bad for what I had done. But in that moment, I felt safe. I believed him when he said that we would work everything out. But I also knew that working everything out was going to be a long and difficult process.

"What happens now?" Aunt Sandy asked Mrs. Green.

"My safety agents and I will meet with the police and give them a full report. They are also going to want to speak with each of the students involved. Both of you will have to be in the room with Michael since you are his legal guardians and he is underage. When that's over, you will be free to leave. Tomorrow morning my superintendent will be here to talk about what happened, as well as the consequences for those involved. At that point I will reach out to you at home to let you know."

The conversation was interrupted. "I'm looking for a Mrs. Green," a police officer said, walking toward us.

"Yes, that's me."

"Roger Castle, Chief of Police for District 25. Is there somewhere we can talk?"

Officer Castle's voice gave me chills. It was deep and commanding. But scarier than that was his physical presence. I had never been that close to a police officer before. He had to be 6'4 and must have weighed 230 pounds. His left hand rested on his gun still in the holster and his handcuffs made a clanging sound as he walked toward us. For a brief second we made eye contact. My mind began to wander. All I could see were prison bars and orange jumpsuits. That was the most terrifying image. What the heck would I do if I were shipped off somewhere?

If what I had seen in the movies was true, I was certain I wouldn't be able to spend a day in prison much less a couple of years—which I was sure was the kind of time I would get had I really hurt anyone with that knife. There'd be no school dance, no graduation from middle school and going off to high school, and definitely no chance of ever going back home and reuniting with my friends and family. And Dad, when would I see him again? I would be known as the kid who made a terrible mistake all because he wanted to be popular. I could forget about going to college and becoming an entrepreneur. The bank would never loan me money with a criminal record.

My head was beginning to hurt. I was starting to get a queasy feeling in the pit of my stomach. That was definitely not the life I wanted for myself.

"Thank you for getting here as fast as you did," Mrs. Green said to Officer Castle. "Terribly sorry it's under these circumstances. Please, right this way." She turned to Aunt Sandy. "The three of you can sit in the waiting area until we are ready for you."

And so the process begins! I swallowed. I felt like I was going to be sick.

Walking to the waiting area was horrible. I felt the weight of disappointment on my shoulders. I really let Aunt Sandy and Uncle Carl down. And Mom…I let her down the most. Would I have done any of this if she were still alive? How could I have been so stupid?

I saw a familiar face in the office.

"Hey Roy!" I said. "Waiting your turn?"

He looked up. "Yup. My parents are on their way."

"Where's Tye?"

He motioned to a closed door in the office. "He's in there with them already. His father is irate. He's even talking about taking Tye out of school himself and sending him away."

"Wow!"

"Michael! Come over here and sit down." Aunt Sandy barked.

"Catch up with you later, man." Then I added, "Maybe."

"Later Mike!"

We waited for about thirty minutes. No one said a word; we just waited. I had my head down in my lap, whilst Aunt Sandy sipped a hot cup of coffee. Uncle Carl continued to pace back and forth.

The squeaking sound of a door opening startled us all. It was Tye and his parents.

"I can't believe you would even do something like this," Tye's father said. "I told you that kid Vince was bad news, but you wouldn't listen. Now look what's happened. Let's just hurry up and get to the car. We have a lot to talk about."

Roy's parents still hadn't arrived, so it was our turn.

"You guys can come in now," Mrs. Green said, motioning to Aunt Sandy and Uncle Carl.

I looked at Tye as he walked past, leaving the office. The look on his face was one of deep regret. *It may be some time before I see him again...or any of these guys for that matter.*

"Mr. and Mrs. Peters, this is Officer Castle," Mrs. Green announced. "He is going to ask Michael a few questions and then talk with you both a little about some things. Officer Castle, it's all yours."

"Good afternoon, the officer said in a similar tone to Mrs. Green. I am here to get some information about what took place today. Michael, why don't you start by telling me how you met the other boys. Then you can tell me about what happened today."

The thought of going back to how this all started made my head hurt. But I had to relive all of the poor choices I made to end up in this situation.

I hope I don't have to talk about this ever again.

Talking to Officer Castle made me extremely uncomfortable. I told him everything. There was no sense in lying anymore or holding anything back. But what sucked the most was telling him about taking Uncle Carl's knife and lying to him and Aunt Sandy. We were in that room for about forty minutes.

"Well, I think that just about covers everything. I don't have any more questions for Michael at this time. Do either of you have any questions for me?" Officer Castle said to Aunt Sandy and Uncle Carl.

"Do we have to worry about Michael being charged with anything?" Aunt Sandy asked.

My chest tightened. Here was the moment of truth.

"Well, since he is a minor and he never did anything with the knife, there really isn't much to charge him with," Officer Castle responded. "I wouldn't worry too much."

"But Michael's not getting off completely free," Mrs. Green followed. "He has broken some serious rules just by having a weapon on campus, and by leaving school on Friday when he was forbidden to do so." She turned to look at me.

"You've participated in something that has put several students in danger, including yourself. Because of that, Michael, you're going to be suspended for quite some time." Mrs. Green glanced at Aunt Sandy again. "This is a very serious offense."

Aunt Sandy took a deep breath. "Okay. We understand."

My time was up. It was Roy's turn. His mother finally made it.

"See you later, Roy?" I said, exiting the waiting room.

He gave me a grim look, but his mother looked thoroughly vexed.

The ride home was excruciating. I wondered what was going through Aunt Sandy and Uncle Carl's minds. Were they angry with me? Disappointed? Did they regret looking after Nicky and myself since Mom passed away?

CHAPTER TWELVE
THE AFTERMATH

"Michael! Michael, wake up. We're home," Aunt Sandy said, putting the car in park.

Uncle Carl closed the gate and went straight inside without saying a word.

I opened the car door to get out, pausing, thankful that I wasn't at a hospital or a police station. I wondered how Vince was doing and if I'd ever see him again. I'm sure he'd be in the most trouble since he was the one with a loaded gun.

Aunt Sandy was already out of the car and walking into the house. As I came in, she and Uncle Carl stopped me before I could head up to my room.

"Come and sit for a second, Michael." Aunt Sandy said, pointing to the dining room.

I could tell by the look on their faces that this was bad news.

"We just want you to know that we are extremely relieved that you are okay," Aunt Sandy said as we sat at the table. "We didn't know what to expect when we got the call from your school. But we also want you to know that we are very disappointed in you. We agreed to have you and Nicky live with us for a while until things get sorted out with your father."

Oh no! Did my actions cost Nicky and me the security of being here? Aunt Sandy sounded like she was about to renege the whole deal. With things still unsettled there and Dad still being back and forth with work, I knew that this was the best place for us to be right now. Aunt Sandy and Uncle Carl opened their home to us and now they were about to kick us out.

"...And we are still willing to do that," Aunt Sandy continued.

I breathed a sigh of relief. She saw my relieved expression and glanced at me sternly.

"But something like this can never happen again, Michael. This could have gone really badly and you could have been hurt or even killed. And that would have destroyed us. I can't even imagine what we would have done if the call from your school was to tell us that you had been shot or that you were dead." She swallowed, obviously starting to get choked up. Tears filled her eyes as she pushed through her emotions to continue talking. "We care about you like one of our own. You're basically a son to us," she said, beginning to weep. "We are all family now. This family talks about our issues and how we feel about certain things. Promise us you will never do anything like this again."

My heart raced with guilt. Overwhelmed, I dropped my head into my palms, stricken with embarrassment. To know that I could have caused someone that amount of pain and sorrow was something I'd never felt before. And it was surely something I never wanted to feel again. Even Uncle Carl, someone who maintained a serious and unwavering demeanor, began sniffling and shifting uncomfortably in his seat. I never truly considered how my actions might have affected the people around me. I was so caught up in my own pursuit of popularity, in my own selfish desire to look good and make a name for myself, that the thought of hurting those who cared for me the most was something I pushed to the back of my mind.

With a trembling voice and very little eye contact, I replied, "I am so sorry about everything. I don't know what got into me." I swallowed and spoke slowly so my voice wouldn't crack. "This all happened so fast. I just wanted to be seen with the cool kids. I had no idea that things would get this crazy. But I promise not to let anything like this happen again. From now on I'm going to focus on my schoolwork and find a sport that I like so that I can get involved and stay out of trouble."

Aunt Sandy and Uncle Carl looked at each other, simultaneously taking a deep breath.

Uncle Carl nodded. "Okay. You can go upstairs and get washed up. Dinner will be ready in about an hour."

I nodded and mouthed *"Okay"*, my voice had vanished because of the overwhelming emotion.

Walking away, I felt a sense of relief. Uncle Carl and Aunt Sandy seemed to understand, even though they were both upset. I wasn't sure Mom would have been this lenient. Then again, I wasn't sure any of this would have happened if she were still here.

I just wanted to get up to my room and lie down. There was so much to think about. I'd be thinking about the last week and a half for a very long time.

***

By the time I got up to my room I had calmed myself down a little. I plopped down on the bed so I could relax and tune out for a while. Not so lucky. Ten minutes later, there was a knock at the door.

"Michael, you in there?" It was Nicky.

"Yeah."

She opened the door and gave me a stern look. "Lying, stealing a knife and taking it to school? Skipping school to fight a battle that was not yours? Seriously, Michael! What the heck is wrong with you?"

I sighed. "I guess you heard." I looked up at the ceiling.

"Yes I heard. What are you trying to do? Get us shipped back home where we'd be in a much worse situation?"

I sat up. "No I'm not trying to do that!" My temper suddenly flared. "I made a mistake, okay? And I'm sorry for it. Haven't you ever made a mistake? You're the one who wanted to be here in the first place, not me. Maybe a part of me subconsciously did all this so we *would* be sent back home, I don't know. But what I do know is that I made a mistake, a stupid one. And last time I checked, I wasn't perfect. So lay off, Nicky. I feel bad enough as it is without you getting in my face."

Nicky instantly noticed that I was extremely upset.

She took a deep breath to calm down, and leaned back with her arms folded. I threw my head back and hit the bed, staring back at the ceiling.

"Look, I know you're still dealing with the fact that Mom is gone and we're stuck here for a while," she said quietly. "I know you're hurting inside and that you might even be angry."

She took my hands and held them tight, even after I tried to pull them away. "But you can't do stuff like this. This is not the kind of attention you want. It will only make things worse for you and for all of us."

"I know. I got the lecture from Aunt Sandy and Uncle Carl already."

"So this won't happen again?"

"No! It won't!"

"Good!" Nicky stood up, turning to walk out of my room. I don't think she really wanted to talk about it much either. Maybe I was a little hard on her. But I'd had just about enough of today.

A few seconds later, she returned. "You know I love you, right?"

"I know, sis. Love you too."

I breathed. Finally, some time to myself to get some rest and forget about today.

Or so I thought. It wasn't long before Cole and Jake were knocking at the door.

"Come in."

"What's up cousin?" Jake said, walking in, Cole right behind him.

"Hey." I was exhausted, and it was clear from my tone. I hoped it would be a signal to them that I didn't want to be bothered.

"We heard about the lockdown at your school. What happened?" Jake asked.

Guess that didn't work.

I took in a deep breath. After talking to Nicky, I thought I would get away from telling this story for the rest of today. But part of me didn't mind talking to Cole and Jake. Maybe it was because we are a similar age. But somehow we ended up talking about everything for a while. Well, it was really me who did most of the talking.

"You're crazy! I could never do anything like that," Cole said after I told them everything.

"Punk! I would!" Jake replied, trying to show up his brother.

Cole scoffed. "No you wouldn't! Dad would kill you."

"Obviously he wouldn't know. Duh!"

Cole rolled his eyes, giving up. "Whatever! We're just glad you're okay, Mike. This could have gone completely left."

"Yeah cuz! You have to make sure that you hang with the right people here–people who are trying to achieve something positive in life. Sounds like Vince and his crew are just the opposite," Jake said.

He was right. Andrew and Matt popped into my head. *Wonder how they're going to react when I see them again*, I thought. Then I corrected myself: *If I see them again*. I still didn't know what the school was going to do. I may never go back there.

"Boys, come downstairs and get washed up for dinner please. We are sitting down in ten minutes," Aunt Sandy yelled.

"Coming!" Cole replied.

Now that everyone in the house knew what happened, I felt the weight of guilt and shame fall off my shoulders. I felt a sense of ease. I didn't have to hide anything or lie anymore like I had for the past couple of weeks. I think that caused me more stress than anything else.

Dinner was a little awkward at first but then Cole asked about Uncle Carl's fishing trip and that became the topic of conversation. Apparently, he caught his biggest fish to date. When dinner was over, all I wanted to do was take a shower and hit the sack. Today was probably one of the longest and most overwhelming days of my life.

***

It was 8:36 a.m. on Tuesday morning. Cole and Jake had already left for school hours ago. I made sure I turned my alarm clock off the night before because I knew I wasn't going to school today. But the sun beaming into my room was unavoidable. It hit me straight in the face, waking me up out of the best sleep I had since coming here. I wanted nothing more than to lie down again and go back to sleep for another hour or so, but I had to use the bathroom.

The phone rang as I was exiting the attic stairwell.

"Hello, good morning!" Aunt Sandy answered.

A pause.

"Oh hello, Mrs. Green."

"Mrs. Green?" I said under my breath. I knew this call was coming, but I didn't think I would be around to hear it.

I stood on the last step to hear Aunt Sandy's part of the conversation, but I could only hear pieces since she was still in her room.

I couldn't hold on any longer. I gave up on listening to her one-sided conversation and went to the bathroom.

"Michael, is that you?" Aunt Sandy asked as I flushed the toilet.

"Yes, it's me."

"Come on down to the kitchen when you're finished, please. Your uncle and I have to speak with you."

It was sentencing time. I'm sure that's what that conversation was about. Mrs. Green must have met with the superintendent.

"Good morning," I said, nervously walking into the kitchen to see Uncle Carl and Aunt Sandy.

"Morning," they replied.

"I just got off the phone with your principal," Aunt Sandy said. "She met with the superintendent and they have come up with what they feel is the best solution."

I inhaled deeply and said, "So what's it going to be?"

"They are going to give you in-house suspension for three weeks with a note to your file. During those three weeks, you will report to one designated room where all of your classwork will be brought to you as well as your lunch. You will stay there for the entire day except for gym class."

"Three weeks in one room? That sounds like a jail cell." I replied.

"It's the only choice you have right now, son," Uncle Carl said.

"And this is much lighter than what they wanted to do originally, which was to transfer you to another school," Aunt Sandy went on. "But Mrs. Green vouched for you. She told the superintendent about what happened with your mother and how this move hasn't been easy for you."

I had no words. The thought of having to be in one room for seven periods was ridiculous. But I guess Aunt Sandy was right. This could be worse. I couldn't imagine having to start all over at another school this far into the year.

"Now that's just for school. You are also facing some consequences at home as well."

"Oh man! What are those?" I said, hanging my head. I knew this was coming too. I was hoping maybe they would have mercy on me, but I guess I deserved it.

"You're grounded for the next month. No video games, no phone calls, and no company. You can only leave the house when you are going to school and if we are all going out somewhere as a family. And you will double up on some chores around here. Understood?"

"Yes ma'am."

"Since you will be home today, you can get started on some of those chores. After you have your breakfast, please vacuum the living room and clean the upstairs bathroom."

"Yes ma'am."

This was going to be a long month. Why did I agree to any of this nonsense with Vince and the others? All of this for popularity? This was so not worth it.

***

158

When Wednesday morning came, I was excited for school. I was up and dressed before Cole and Jake were ready.

Cole came downstairs first. When he saw me ready to go, he did a double take.

"You're up and ready pretty early. And you actually seem eager for school," Cole said, confused.

"Actually, I am."

"But we heard about your suspension. You can't be that excited."

"I'm just ready to get this all over with."

"You are?" Jake asked, jumping off the last step.

"Yeah, I am. I realized something since I had so much time to think yesterday."

"What's that?" Cole said.

"I realized that I didn't become popular in Trinidad by trying to be accepted by the cool kids. I became popular be just being myself and doing the things that I liked. More than one person told me to do that here but I didn't listen. And look where it got me. I'm not a fighter. I never carried weapons to school. And I never cut class before in my life. I did all of this for someone I hardly knew and for a fight that wasn't mine to begin with. I became someone I was never meant to be, for all the wrong reasons. And it only got me into trouble, and almost killed. From now on, I'm just going to be me. And whoever wants to be my friend is welcome. Because at the end of the day, none of those guys would care if I was locked up or six feet under."

Cole and Jake looked at each other, impressed.

"That's pretty deep cuz!' Jake said.

"I second that!" Cole said.

On the bus, I had just minutes before I had to face the music. I wanted to get everything over with...but was I really ready?

I was extremely nervous about walking into school, more than ever before.

"Hey, Mike! Is that you?" A familiar voice settled my nerves.

It was Andrew. He and Matt had just gotten off another bus and were walking in behind me.

"Hey guys. What's up?" I was relieved to see them. I couldn't tell if they felt the same way about seeing me, though. Not yet.

"Nothing much. We didn't think we would see you back this soon."

"They gave me in-house suspension for three weeks."

"Three weeks? That's a long time to be in one room," Matt said.

"Yeah," I agreed. "But it's better than being cooped up in the house all day. My aunt has me on lockdown too–no games, phone or company. *And* she gave me more housework. So trust me, being here is much better."

They nodded, not saying anything.

"Listen, I owe the two of you an apology," I went on. "You tried to warn me and I didn't listen. The whole time I thought I was looking for better friends, not realizing that I had two great ones the whole time. Thanks for trying to help me, even though I ignored you. Now I don't know if you guys still want to be friends or not, but I'm keen if you are."

There was an awkward pause, followed by a soft giggle shared between Andrew and Matt.

"What the heck is so funny?"

"Of course we're still friends, bro," Andrew said.

"Yeah we think you learned your lesson," Matt added.

I joined in their laughter.

"Okay cool. I'll catch up with you guys later in gym class. My only time of freedom for the next three weeks," I said, rolling my eyes.

"Later bro!" Andrew said.

I made my way to the front office, as instructed.

"Mr. Bell! Good morning. Nice to have you back. Although much sooner than I expected. You must have an angel watching over you," said Agent Connolly. He would be escorting me and the other in-house suspension students to our room for the day.

"Good morning, Agent Connolly," I said. "Where are Tye and Roy? Didn't they get the same suspension as me?"

"No sir," he said. "Roy got transferred to another school about ten miles from here. It's a school for troubled teens. Tye's father sent him to live with his grandmother in Georgia. He thinks a change of environment would be best. And Vince…well, he won't be coming back either. He'll be away for a while if you know what I mean."

"Wow!" I said, amazed. I couldn't believe what I had just heard. Compared to the others, I had gotten off easy—*very* lucky even. *Mom must really be looking out for me.*

"Is that Michael?"

That was a voice I knew too well.

"Good morning, Mrs. Green," I said turning around.

"Let me have a word with you." She turned to Agent Connolly. "Would you mind waiting for a moment?"

"Not at all, ma'am."

Mrs. Green stepped to the side of her doorway, motioning me in.

I wasn't sure what to expect. Was she going to lecture me on her expectations of me going forward? Was she going to say how lucky I was that she vouched for me with the superintendent? Or was she just happy to see me?

"So how are you feeling now that you are back?" she asked in a transparent tone as we reached her office.

"Fine I guess."

"You guess? Surely you've taken some time over the last couple of days to think about the extent of your negligent behavior." She looked at me seriously.

I paused. Mrs. Green had a way with words—she made me think for a moment. I had to make sure I responded correctly so that this conversation didn't go south.

"I did. And I realized the error in my ways. My priorities were definitely out of order and that caused me to lose sight of what I should really be focusing on."

"Which is what?" she prompted.

"My schoolwork and making something of myself. Something positive."

She smiled, obviously pleased with my answer. "That's right, Michael. From the first day I met you, I knew there was something different about you. There was an interesting sense of curiosity that shadowed you when we were walking to class on your first day. The way you looked around and the way you carried yourself. I could tell that your mother did a good job raising you to be respectful and humble. That's why I was so surprised that you were involved in all of this mess."

She leaned forward.

"I want you to check in with me every week going forward. I won't tell you when, because I want you to be responsible enough to make sure you do. Can you do that for me?"

I nodded, grateful for everything. "Yes ma'am."

"I'm going to be watching you, Michael. I believe in you and I'm here for you if you need me."

"Thank you."

I wasn't going to mess this up again. *These people actually care about me. I'll never let them down again.*

"Agent Connolly," Mrs. Green said, standing and walking around her giant wooden desk.

"Come on, this way," Agent Connolly instructed me, pointing down the hall.

While walking down the hall, we passed Miss Smith's office. Her door was open, and I poked my head in.

"Hi Miss Smith."

"Michael!" she said in a surprised but happy tone. "I heard about everything that happened a couple days ago. How are you doing?"

"Well, that's what I was hoping I could talk to you about. Could you ask Mrs. Green if you can still pull me out of class even though I'm on suspension? I think I'm ready to speak with you now."

A smile spread across her face. "I will walk over there and ask her right now, Michael. I think she'll be fine with that."

"Okay. Thank you."

"Mr. Bell! Keep it moving please," Agent Connolly barked.

I ran up to catch the line of students entering the classroom. I wasn't too happy about how everything had played out over the last few days. That was in the past and there was no one to blame but myself. Now, I knew that my actions were the result of something deeper. And I was ready to talk about that with Miss Smith.

Made in the USA
Lexington, KY
28 October 2019